THE "MAGPIE COFFIN"

WILE E. YOUNG

DEATH'S HEAD PRESS

an imprint of Dead Sky Publishing, LLC
Miami Beach, Florida
www.deadskypublishing.com

ISBN: 9781639510382

Cover Art: Justin T. Coons

The "Splatter Western" logo designed
by K. Trap Jones

Book Layout: Lori Michelle
www.TheAuthorsAlley.com

FOR DAD, THE ORIGINAL
GOOD, BAD, AND UGLY.

ACKNOWLEDGMENTS

Thank you to Jarod Barbee and Patrick Harrison at Death's Head Press for continuing to ride with this young gun.

My gratitude goes out to my wife, Emily, who has ridden with me through the best, helped me escape the noose, and always told me when I was riding on a high horse.

I would like to thank a few lawmen, renegades, and bounty hunters who've helped and supported me: Brian Keene, Stephen Kozeniewski, Mary San Giovanni, Bob Ford, Kelli Owen, Somer Canon, Wesley and Katie Southard, Mike Lombardo, Linda Addison, and a long list of others.

CHAPTER ONE

A **MIGHTY THUNDERSTORM** rolled in the night I heard.

I immediately sat up in the bed. Furnace, Texas wasn't known for getting storms out of season; the dry heat and rattlesnake holes up on the Boot Hill made it seem like Hell's waiting room. Thunderbolts flashed down from the heavens, rain splattered against the window.

The temptation to reach for my weapon scratched at my mind like the prick of a scorpion's tail. My hand was downright trembling and the gun lying on the dresser whispered sweet words in my ears. It was like an itch; ten years of paranoia had wound me tight and I didn't feel comfortable unless the weapon was in my hand.

They were coming, always had been, ever since Centralia.

I listened to the wind and rain pound against the pane, my eyes flicking back and forth between the door and the window. Nothing was coming, nothing moved. If Fate had plans for me tonight, she was sure as shit taking her time.

A sigh escaped the woman in bed with me, her

auburn hair spilling out around her on the blankets. For a moment, I thought about lying back down and enjoying the rest of the night I'd paid her for.

An old teacher's words came to me: 'Ignoring signs will lead you to death, gun or not.' There wouldn't be any more shuteye for me. Not tonight.

I gently left the bed. Scouting back in the war and my time with the People had lent me plenty of skill in the art of silence.

I adjusted my belt of ammunition, along with the Bowie knife, and picked up the Gun. The revolver's ivory grip felt warm in my hand and the demon's sign that had been engraved there pressed into my skin.

I didn't have to look to know it was loaded.

The woman never even moved as I stacked the two gold quarter eagles on the nightstand. I was halfway out the room before I turned around and pulled a small bag of red velvet from my pocket. The hoodoo work wasn't as well done as my teacher's. Old Louisiane Robichaude would have put a working on me if she'd seen the low-quality ingredients I was using, but it would do just fine. I whispered the words, just like I'd been taught, then I left it under her pillow.

Anyone came calling for me, they'd be warned off, 'less she brought attention to herself and then her fate was in the Good Lord's hands.

I never looked back.

Furnace was like most towns with the saloon right across the street from the hotel where I had been enjoying my company. Maestro and Soldier were stabled up the road along with the old stagecoach I made my travels in. Wish I'd had the foresight to bring myself a timepiece. Felt like the witching hour in my bones.

Even through the din of noise I could see the light and laughter spilling out of the building. My footsteps echoed as I pushed my way in, hat soaking as it dripped onto the floor.

It was full of Yankee men, celebrating about some such or another, dressed out in their blues and drinking away the night. I'd seen them ride in around sunset, but I'd kept to the shadows. Wanted posters after the war might have been a memory, but I wasn't one to take chances, especially with Jesse and his bunch still causing trouble up north. Probably helped that I'd made sure never to take a photograph and most folks who had known me were dead.

I stalked through the saloon, heading toward the bar. I draped myself over it and signaled for a shot of whiskey. A flash of coin and the ugly liquid was put in front of me. I downed it and signaled for another. The bar man came close and, as he sat the bottle in front of me, I asked him the question that was burning me.

"What're they celebrating?"

The bartender glanced at my face, but that was enough for him to recognize me. His eyes widened and he went white like the ghosts they said haunted the boot hill. I had myself a distinguishing feature, you see, a brand that took up most of the flesh beneath my left eye. Wasn't disfiguring, I chewed my grits same as any other man, just let folks know that when my time came, I wasn't going to be walking through those pearly gates.

WILE E. YOUNG

"I asked you a question. Rude not to answer."

His hand twitched under the bar. "I'm not looking for trouble, people just want to celebrate. Indian Wars are over . . . Quanah surrendered up at Fort Sill two days ago."

My face was impassive, but my heart turned cold in my chest. I'd been fighting most of my life for one thing or another, but to hear my last teacher's people had finally given up the ghost was a blow I knew I'd be dealing with in the coming days.

I examined the whiskey bottle in front of me, sighing heavily. "Friend, you know who I am. That peacemaker you have back there won't help you." I turned my head so I could look into his eyes, get the full measure of him and maybe share a bit of soul while it was still mine. "I can't be killed by a gun." With that, I poured myself another shot and didn't give the man another thought.

The bullet never came. When next I looked, the man was at the other end of the bar, trying not to let the rest of the crowd see his gooseflesh or fidgeting hands.

One of the Yankee soldiers slammed into the bar to my right. I ignored him, concentrating on my own thoughts, wondering how my last teacher was taking the surrender of his people.

"It's a good night, friend, a good night for damn sure!" He hollered into my ear and I felt his spittle on my face. Out of the mouths of fools comes information.

Quietly, I asked him, "Why is it a good day?"

"Haven't heard? Redskins are through!" His voice was grating, high pitched, like manhood had skipped him over.

4

"That so?" Almost couldn't bring myself to believe it, not with my teacher's ways. He knew enough big medicine that even with my gun I wouldn't have placed myself ahead in a fight.

"Killing the buffalo herds is what done 'em. Good folks like you done their part and us killing the rest . . . just done 'em in good!" His shout echoed off the saloon walls and his five compatriots cheered. The other patrons, maybe seven in all, followed suit.

"Congratulations." It was a dry remark, intended for this horse turd to leave me drowning in my whiskey. But Fate has a way getting you where she needs.

"Wish I could have been with that Bad Hand Outfit, bagging themselves a white one!"

My blood ran cold and my voice eased into a whisper. "What?"

The man grinned, eager to tell his story. "Oh yeah, sons of bitches were ambushed up at Palo Duro Canyon. Bunch escaped, of course, but five of his scouts tracked down some medicine man who was protecting a white buffalo." The soldier snickered as I stared unblinking out of the corner of my right eye; whiskey had gone to his head and he was oblivious to my fury.

"Savage was praying some witchcraft or another the whole time when they caught up with him. Shot the big white bastard right through the head. Way I heard it was that it had markings all over it, like some kind of heathen scripture . . . devil worship or some such." The Yankee sighed like he was recounting some dream he'd had on the plains. "The redskin collapsed after that, from what I heard. Screamed all kinds of hell 'til the scouts killed him too . . . slit his throat for all his hollering."

I passed the whiskey bottle to the man and he nodded. "Thank you kindly, friend. Forgot to tell the strangest thing . . . " He uncorked the bottle and stared into the brown liquid swirling beneath. "Spoke some English at the end. Said plainly, 'Black Magpie will come.' The soldier took a swig of the whiskey and sighed deeply, his eyes wide and wondering. "That's what they called the boy who ran with Quantrill up in Kansas, the one those rebels were all superstitious about . . . " I turned in my seat. The kid saw the mark under my left eye and froze.

When Fate flips the cards, calls your chips, it's always unexpected.

The Gun was already in my hand; hadn't been aware I was reaching for it. Smoke and thunder roared and the glass in the Yankee's hands exploded. My aim was never off. The bullet had found his eye, blood pouring from the liquefied remains of his socket.

He tumbled off the chair and I was already turning on his companions. They were drunk, stumbling and crashing to raise themselves from the table where they'd been gambling away their money.

I took my time, cold fury in every bullet. I emptied the five chambers on two men. Dark maroon blossomed under the first man's blues as his heart futilely tried to pump life through him. A dark stain spread through his trousers; he hadn't even tried to shoot.

His companion had found both his kneecaps were now a shattered mess of blood and bone. He screamed like a woman in birth.

They don't tell you how they scream, how it warms the soul.

Most patrons were spilling out into the night or trying to turn tables upright so I wouldn't see them, but not the three remaining soldiers. A brown-haired mouse of a man fired, but it went wild and shattered a bottle sitting behind me. I walked forward as his companion fired and the wood in front of my foot splintered.

I walked forward.

The third man had managed to point it at my chest before I knocked him to the floor with a fist. Two rotted teeth and a smattering of blood stained the floor as I stepped hard onto his head, hearing the keening wail under me, his skull caving in with a wet crunch that I felt under my boot.

The last two weren't but two feet away and their panicked shots flew in all directions. Then their guns were spent, their hammers falling on nothing.

My knife found a heart beneath the nearest man's chest. His gurgled cry escaped his mouth as the blood fountained up his throat and ran down his chin. I listened to it like a sweet lullaby before I let him topple to the floor.

The last Yankee tried to run, but my knife found his back and with a grunt he fell ass over head outside into the storm.

Dust settled, the smell of black powder taking me back to distant battlefields. Memory wouldn't be complete without the screaming.

The soldier rolled around, grasping at his kneecaps, sobbing like a newborn babe desperate for Mama's tit. I stepped over him. I could see my reflection in his eye, a black specter covered in other men's blood.

"Your friend told me about the albino buffalo and the shaman your boys killed. His name was Dead Bear. He was my teacher." I spoke it matter-of-factly, spoke it truthfully, no malice in my voice . . . that would come for others.

The man still spat vitriol at me. "Go to hell!"

My boots were stained in the man's blood but I reached down and grasped his head, pulling him close. "I'm going to kill you, but how terrible it is will be up to you. You tell me the names of the men who killed my teacher and in return you won't scream."

In the end he told me, they always did. He didn't scream. The same could not be said for his companion when I retrieved my knife.

CHAPTER TWO

IT WAS TWO days' ride to Fort Sill. I spent most of it in contemplation, watching the signs as my wagon trundled across well-worn paths. It'd been overcast ever since I'd left Furnace, odd thing for this blasted land in July.

Dead Bear had always been in tune with the weather, read the signs in the heavens easy as most folks read the Good Book. He'd blessed the Comanche with his predictions, conditions for hunting, weather to preclude pursuit by the U.S. Army. The old shaman had always stood by his power.

Maestro and Soldier pulled at their reins, my collection rattling around inside the old stagecoach. It was odds and ends mostly, mystical trinkets, and a few body parts from folks I'd found most noteworthy. The scalps of the soldiers from the saloon were the newest addition. I'd hung them off the old railing, listening to the slap of flesh against the wooden door with every bump in the winding road.

I suppose I would use them eventually, before they rotted. The flesh of a man was potent for some things just as it was valuable for others.

Couldn't rightly come into Fort Sill with parts of

dead men hanging off my coach, that wouldn't do. Didn't know if they'd brought my teacher's body back here, either.

So, I watched and listened.

Soldiers are rigid in their thinking, probably the reason I hadn't gone about enlisting for Dixie back in the war. Partisan work had been easier; Quantrill had respected my unique talents and the Devil knew that I'd whipped his boys into a rage easy enough.

Cavalrymen rode by at their determined intervals, easy enough to avoid. Darkness was my ally, this I had been promised long ago and I moved through it as comfortably as any man would through daylight.

I crept silently until I saw the campfires of the people, the sounds of '*numu tekwapu*' spoken amongst them. Quanah's people, Dead Bear's people, some of my last friends.

The guards stood at attention, but I passed between them like bitter wind from something long dead. When I entered the tent, conversation stopped. Even if I was relieved to see them, there were no smiles or happiness. They'd been crushed and they knew it.

"Black Magpie has come, just as we knew he would when we saw the storm." It was not Quanah; I had hoped to speak with him, but this man would also do.

"Is he here, Grandfather? His body?" I asked my question in their language. I was out of practice and it was crude, but they understood me.

The man waved his hand at me dismissively. "Evil spirits take you both and be done. He is not here. They left his body where it fell, west."

My temper was kindled and my hand dropped to my Gun, trembling as it wrapped around the grip, sweat furrowing my brow. The old Comanche didn't try to run, he knew it would be no use to him. He just looked away, as did the others. "Kill me and add my flesh to your collection. The evil ones have hold over you, son of darkness."

I didn't kill him. Instead, I stood and bowed my head. "What about the men that killed him? Are they here?"

None of them spoke, none of them looked at me. I don't blame them; the People had a long memory when their teachings were perverted.

Especially since I was wearing the evidence of that perversion on my hip.

I left the tent after that; there wasn't anything left to say or ask. They would not answer my questions with anything other than contempt.

I would need to seek my answers another way.

The two were smoking pipes on the edge of the camp, their fire burning bright and their laughter reverberating across the night. No need to be subtle anymore, the war was over, the enemy crushed and humiliated.

The plains that were so full of life, millions strong once, were silent.

They looked of sufficient rank to know whom I sought. But I only needed one.

Left or right, that was the choice. It was a heavy feeling, addicting. Killing had always come natural, and damn if it didn't send gooseflesh prickling down my spine at the thought. Especially when it came to those who had humiliated people seeking to live their own way of life.

The one on the right had a thick beard—though he was thinking about shaving it; too many of his compatriots compared it to old General Jackson's own. He was married, had two sons back in Fort Smith, one a few years into schooling and the other on the verge of his seventeenth birthday. I listened to his story in the darkness, memorizing the facets and intricacies of this life, collecting the information just like I collected everything else.

The right man's wife, the mother of his children, was addicted to laudanum, took it for her nerves, but her habits had started to become a burden and his military salary just wasn't providing enough.

The left man was younger; he'd joined up after the war. His father was a cobbler back in New York and he had a sweetheart down in Texas, little senorita close to the Mexican border. He hated the Indians, hated their stench and their looks, claimed that even their physiology was just different enough to prove that God had made them for the express purpose of subjugation.

"Only way they are going to survive, I tell you. Accept a proper way of life, live like us God-fearing Christians. It's over now, though. Just like it was over for the damn Rebels." The older man laughed, clapped the younger on the back, and agreed.

More listening, more debating. The older man was

named Joe. He was looking forward to rearing and training horses back in Arkansas when he mustered out. His older son had a sweetheart that he was looking to marry, and Joe looked forward to the girl dropping a few pups that he could dote on.

His dreams and desires echoed off of me as I pressed my knife against his throat when he drank from his canteen. My knife dug deep and his throat opened. Blood that was nearly black poured out of his throat and I stepped around him, listening to the beautiful whistling as he tried to scream.

"SON OF A BITCH!" The younger man fumbled for his rifle. He managed to turn it around in time for my fist to find him. I felt the bone crunch underneath my knuckles and the young man's already panicked breathing became a high-pitched wail. I wrenched the rifle out of his hand, watching as the twin streams of blood ran from his ruined nose and splattered into his hands, fresh tears marking his baby cheeks.

Satisfied that he wasn't going to be stirring up any more trouble, I turned back to the man that I had murdered. Joe was in the process of passing on, his breathing came out in ragged little whistles as his hands weakly pawed at his throat, trying to close it. His long beard was matted and wet, the black pool of blood still bubbling out of him every time he took a choked and gurgling breath.

I reached down and lifted his head, an old habit that I indulged in from time to time, watching a man pass. Pearly gates or sulfur rivers, I'd never been able to tell what came afterward, but it felt like the closest I'd ever come to the divine, watching them step into the dark.

Joe's head made a wet noise as I released it back into the dirt. I turned my eyes back to the younger man. He'd managed to find his feet, and was making a run back to the fort. He wasn't far off and, when he found my hands wrapping around his mouth and a crushed up working being shoved down his throat, he didn't even have time to scream.

The sun had risen high by the time he came to and he went to caterwauling almost immediately. Of course, there was no one around to hear him.

We were close to the Texas Panhandle now. I'd lit out from Fort Sill and headed west, letting the winds and whispers guide me. The wilderness was like a sea, flat land dotted with hints of wiry scrub and the smell of rotting meat.

Buffalo carcass dotted the land; the Yankees had done their work well. I remembered the endless herds, the sound of distant thunder as they stampeded across the land. Never to come again, just bleached bones and empty land.

I reined in Soldier and Maestro, both horses stamping their feet in irritation; the man's muffled screams were putting them on edge. Dust billowed as my boots hit the ground and my coach rocked as the man inside struggled with his bonds.

He squinted at the sudden surge of sunlight. I must've struck a sight, like a shadow that had torn itself away and stood between him and the sun. The dust from the working I'd shoved down his throat the previous night powdered his face, thick globs of saliva dribbled down his chin onto his wrinkled uniform.

This wasn't the first time that I'd had someone trussed up in my traveling home. The results were near the same every time. It was the shrunken heads they saw first, twirling down from the canopy by their hair. If you listened close, you could almost hear them whispering. Then there were the vials of blood sloshing around the inside of their bottles, sheriff stars and rank insignias I'd taken from the men I'd killed clinking together.

The odds and ends of my being, my collection of death.

The young man began to scream as he saw it, and I wrapped one fist around his uniform and pulled him into the dirt.

He whimpered as I stood over him, pressing my spur to his neck. "Be quiet."

I could already hear the whispering from my hip, the urge. Another man had been guided into my hand and all I had to do was let loose and the bullet would end his life.

The man wisely took my advice. Light blue eyes that were almost grey looked up at me, the small scrabble of facial hair telling his age.

"Do you know who I am?" It was a fair question, even with the brand scarred under my eye. After all, I'd kept fairly quiet after the war.

"Yes, yes sir. You're a wanted man, killed a lot of sol—"

I pressed the spur deeper into his neck, silencing him and drawing a small trickle of blood. It wasn't hard to get a read on the boy's mind; he knew that

Joe's body had probably been discovered. The scouts would have found my tracks, and the U.S. Army was bearing down on us now. All he had to do was keep me talking and the rescue would come.

I glanced up at the roof of my stagecoach, at my cargo. "If you move or run, I'll kill you. I've got something I reckon you should see."

The answers I needed could be gotten alive or dead, but it was easier if they were still drawing breath. I clambered up onto the stagecoach and looked over the oak coffin I had picked up from a grave man in Fort Hunter. It had been carved from an old gallows tree. I never thought I'd have to go about using it, but some men that I knew wouldn't rest easy.

The smell hit me first when I threw open the lid; riding all night through barren territory attracted all sorts of scavengers and flies flew over the dead man's face and throat. I tipped the coffin on its side and the meat that had once been called Joe flopped out onto the ground. The young man screamed as it thudded into the dirt and oozed black blood into the soil.

"That was your friend, Joe. He has a widow and two sons back east. He was worried about his pay and how he was going to support them, but now he's meat, an offering for coyotes, buzzards, and flies. Now, you have a senorita you're itching to see down in Querido, you hate the People, and your father is a cobbler. These are the only things I will remember about you if you don't give me what I want."

The young man's eyes never left the two dark holes that I had opened in Joe's head, taking his eyes. A lot could be done with a man's eyes if you knew how. Those two dark holes had robbed the young man of speech; even now the buzzing flies crawled in and out of the two pits.

"The scouts will find the tracks, but they'll declare both of you AWOL. Joined up with an outfit eager to find their fortune, I've seen them do it plenty. If they find you, they'll hang you, simple as that." I let that knowledge sink in, wondering how long it was going to take before the fake nobility and courage leaked out of him and I was left with the real man who didn't want to take a ride on the old neck swing.

Then I made my offer. "You ride with me, help me find the men who killed my teacher, you will walk away from this with a pocket of gold and your life. This I swear to you."

The young man's eyes flicked between me and the meat rotting under the sun, maybe he knew that another corpse would keep Joe's company if he refused, maybe he decided that my offer had merit.

It mattered little to me, but when the young man's head nodded and the promise passed over his lips, I cut the bonds that bound him, both in body and soul. I offered him a hand and helped him to his feet. He shakily stood, wiping the dust from his rumpled uniform and smiled shakily. "Thank you, Mr. Covington, thank y—"

I didn't wait for him to finish; daylight was burning and I hoped to reach my destination before dark. Clambering up onto the stagecoach, I flicked the reins and sent Soldier and Maestro into motion. The young man stared bug-eyed for a moment before he hurried after me, scrambling to get on as the horses picked up speed.

As he sat next to me trying to catch his breath, I

asked the only question I cared to know. "What's your name?"

"Jake," He panted. "Jake Howe."

CHAPTER THREE

THE LIGHT WAS just a sliver in the night sky by the time we reached the slaughter.

Jake Howe had given me the names of the men, this Bad Hand Outfit, and told me about their lives. I had listened quietly, soaking in the names of the men I meant to put under the earth.

John Maddox was a tall man, just a little bit shorter than President Lincoln. He was a mick, come all the way over from Ireland in search of riches on the frontier and had learned his trade in the shadows of Liverpool, cracking the skulls of thieves and dodgers.

David Weber and his brother, George, who they called "Sly Eye", were sharpshooters from Kentucky. George was able to pick off a running squaw at one hundred yards, and James was a famous patron at every whorehouse he bothered to frequent. Legend around the unit was that he never had to pay for his pleasures; he could charm and scalp in equal measure.

Then there was Sergeant Earnest Craft. I had heard of him by reputation in the war. He practiced the 'bloody craft' of torture and killing, trying to find new ways to create pain. He'd come up for promotion time and again, but he was too addicted to killing to try for something so civilized.

And last, the one that had sent chills running up my spine when Jake Howe had whispered his name on the long prairie, was Captain August Lamb, the Night Rider himself. I'd heard of this man. After the war, he had testified against the conditions in Andersonville, had spoken of the things he had to do for him and his to survive. That's why they called him the 'Night Rider'; he'd managed to pass through the guards and walls without fail, night after night. From what I'd heard, they'd never bothered to question where he found the meat he brought back.

Jake Howe described these men to me, their personalities, their habits. I absorbed every detail like a rag wiping up spilt oil. When he was finished, I only had one question on my mind.

"Would you know these men if you saw them? Know their faces?" My companion said that he would, just like I'd thought.

We reached the edge of a hill that looked down into a valley, the edge of sweet green grass and the trickle of moving water speaking of its paradise.

The rank smell of rot spoke of death.

Lights danced down in the darkness like fireflies vying to replace the moon in its absence. I clambered into the dirt and sliding gravel, my hand on the Gun, strangely silent as I stared into the valley. Another pair of legs joined me on the ground as Jake followed my lead.

"Watch the horses and retrieve the coffin. Lay it on the ground next the carriage." Jake followed in my wake as I retrieved the scalps of the men I had killed in Furnace. The flies had made their homes among the bloody scraps. The smell that I had grown accustomed to had kept him on the verge of sickness.

"You sure you don't need someone to watch your back? There might be savages or wolves. Hell, with all the stories I've heard about you, it—"

"If you wish to keep your tongue, I would advise you never to call them savages again."

Jake's hand fell to the pistol I had given him, a single action revolver. It was an automatic reflex, one of a man who hadn't learned the new state of things. One glance from me and his hand fell away from it. He kicked dust with his boots and wiped at his cap, his eyes hard and hateful.

"You said that you wouldn't kill me if I helped you. I've heard a lot of things, but they all say that you keep your word. You'd break that over an insult?"

Jake Howe was savvy, this I understood. He wasn't directly challenging me, but he wasn't exactly rolling over, either. I slung the scalps over my coat, the wet slap against my back giving me a dark joy. "I promised I wouldn't kill you and you'd leave with gold in your pocket. If I cut out your tongue, you'll still be alive."

He paled under the moonlight. I walked past him, hand at my side and called back to him, "Get to it, boy."

The darkness swallowed me as I slid down the gravel and shale, keeping a tight hold of the scalps that I had brought. I drew the Gun at my side; the smell of blood was heavy, and where there was death there were things just as eager to eat.

There wasn't any light, but I didn't bother to bring a lantern or a torch; such things had a way of attracting critters that would have liked nothing better than to feast on my entrails.

My heart was beating something fierce. I could see the bobbing lights ahead like they were men trying to find their way out of a dense fog. I ignored them; they weren't men and I wasn't eager to see where they would lead me.

Coyote song rang down from somewhere to my right, a small series of yips and howls that let me know that they were close. From somewhere there was squawking, a deep low groan of a bison, excited yowls and yips, hunger being satisfied. All things natural gone mad with the dead ushering them to kill.

I could feel it, the Gun was whispering into my head. I couldn't see the corpses strewn out in this valley but to my weapon it might as well have been clear as day. Shapes moved around me, large, hairy, and something growled. I didn't pay it any mind; I'd put more men in the ground before I'd let a wolf kill me. I moved on.

It wasn't until I spied two dark forms lying on the ground that I stopped, a pair of dead trees that had fallen long ago. Between them was a small cairn of stones. Fate has a way of guiding you where you need to be, and my teacher had known what would attract me better than I did.

I took my place on the log and rested the Gun across my leg. I tried not to twitch as I let my finger fall away from the trigger. It was itching, restless; I hadn't drawn blood with it since Furnace. If anything decided to take me now, the devil would have to set an extra place at dinner tonight.

I struck a match against one of the cairn stones. There was a spark of red and the kindling at its base ignited in dirty red flame. Something big growled in the darkness, a low noise that sent shivers racing over my skin. The distant sound of the dying bison reached one long, pained moan and then fell silent to the sounds of ripping flesh and breaking bone.

Beyond the light of the fire, behind the other log, something large loomed; even hunched it came up to my head, brown fur matted with dried blood, and two glowing eyes that peered out of the darkness.

I'd never been one for fear. I'd done my fair share of killing, seen all the ways that you could kill a man, but looking into the eyes of the massive animal hunkering in the shadows reminded me of what terror felt like. Had to be a bear, only thing that could be that big. Its mouth hung open and a steady stream of hot breath floated into the air. I'd been expecting this, had theories about what it was, could have been wrong or right. Sometimes a bear is just a bear.

The scalps stained my hands with dry blood as I stood and those twin glowing eyes seemed to swivel in that massive skull as they looked at the Gun sitting on the log next to me.

"An offering of meat, white man scalps. I need to speak with you."

The bear didn't respond as I tossed the four pieces of hair and flesh over it and into the dark. Its eyes stared at me for a long time before it gave a long shuddering snort and ambled off into the night.

I sat back down on the log and waited. My mind drifted back to Centralia like it always did, the faces of twenty-two men who hadn't wanted to die. Some of them still screamed from the bottles inside my stagecoach.

We'd won the battle after, sure enough; their scalps had been good enough payment to assure that. That had been for the cause, not my purposes. Causes were for chumps and suckers who believed that the world was carried on angels' wings, and more often than not they'd found a bullet.

Something moved at the edge of the firelight. I had long expected the fire to die down, but whatever kindling my teacher had gathered burned nice and strong. I kept my hand on the Gun as a man stepped out of the night. He was clothed in furs and moccasins. White face paint that gave him the appearance of a dead man stepped right out of the grave. His forehead had been peeled off, scalped in the same way that his people had. Bits of totems and jewelry hung around his neck, still dripping with blood from where his throat had been slit. Two eyes that burned with feral intensity stared into me.

Dead Bear, my teacher.

I raised a hand in peace and he did likewise, unmoving and unspeaking. The Gun didn't whisper for me to shoot, not when there was no more blood to shed. He sat down on the opposite log and stared at me with eyes that were dilated enough that the black nearly touched the edges.

"I've got a buck who knows the lay of things,

collected him in Fort Sill. Expect you know about the things that happened there."

The old shaman didn't answer. The fire glimmered in those eyes, his mouth turned in a deep frown.

From somewhere distant came a deep roar. Coyotes ran with frightened whimpers and the tearing sounds of wet meat came.

"I've collected their stories, their souls are next, for what they did, what else they'll do. I swear this by you, and by my word."

Dead Bear reached over in silence and produced a tomahawk, carving designs in the dirt while his eyes focused in hard, head tilted slightly.

"Things didn't end well between us. I perverted your ways just like I did all the others . . . " I held the Gun out so that he could see. He flinched back, teeth bared. "Same reaction I should have had, but you, Lousianne, old Stoltzfus up in Appalachia, all of you let me learn your craft. That's a debt I've been long overdue in repaying."

I put the Gun back into the holster, picking up a discarded twig and twirling it through the red flames. Now came the risk, the danger I'd be putting myself in along with Jake Howe, though I didn't exactly care about his state as long as he could point out the Bad Hand.

"You're raging, teacher, I can see it plain as day. Sounds like you've killed plenty of varmints, moving onto folks soon, I expect. I'd walk that same path if my sacred herd had been desecrated and I'd been left to bleach under the sun."

Dead Bear's hands gripped the wood, a deep

rumbling growl echoing between those closed lips, wild, eager to sink his teeth into anything. We'd parted on bad terms and he wasn't looking to make amends, but that growl let me know that my blood smelled sweet. A fresh layer of fear to season the bones.

"You can rage until you burn out. Maybe the fire smolders, maybe your anger dies; either way, ain't exactly peaceful. I'm willing to take you, plant you proper, recite all the proper rites of the People. You'll rest easy and free."

The growl in my teacher's throat died away. I'd made my offer, no use trying to sweeten the deal with anything else. I watched, waited, and kept my hand on the Gun.

Dead Bear stood up. I kept my eyes rooted on him. He stumbled a step forward, then another. The tomahawk dragged the ground, destroying the small drawings he'd been crafting in the dirt. He reached out, his skin wrapped so tight around his brown fingers they may as well have been obsidian-stained bone. They brushed the brand underneath my eye, the touch sending a stab of pain, agony that went deeper than the flesh.

Shame runs through the soul and the pain from that don't heal so easy.

My teacher's face came close, his mouth hovered over my ear. I could smell his breath—blood and the raw smell of marrow; dust from where he had been laying ran from between his teeth.

There was no air, the dead didn't breathe, but I heard the word, clear as a death rattle.

"Abandon."

A twig snapped behind me and the fire around the stones snuffed out as I whirled around, the Gun leaving the holster screaming in my head for blood.

I barely avoided pulling the trigger and sending Jake off to the Promised Land. I was breathing heavy, reining in my emotions so that he wouldn't see how rattled I was. The lantern clattered in his gloved hand, his eyes staring at the darkness of the Gun pointed at his face. "Please, Mr. Covington . . . " He swallowed hard, trying not to show how scared he was. "I didn't mean to startle you."

I breathed out, clicking the hammer shut and putting my weapon away. "Thought I told you to watch the horses."

Jake managed to steady his hand, the lantern light falling over the log and stone. "They were spooking heavy. Heard all kinds of noises down here, thought I'd give you some back up . . . then I saw you with the fire, talking to that corpse."

He pointed a finger. Dead Bear wasn't standing by me, wasn't whispering words. He lay belly down in the dirt on the other side of the stones, his mouth hanging open, eyes wide with pain, brown and bloody skull buzzing with flies.

I stood up, reaching out a hand to pet the stone cairn. It was cool to the touch.

Jake spoke up behind me. "What is it?"

"Did you see anyone else here?" I asked. He shook his head swiftly, like he was afraid I'd copy the dead man's wounds onto him.

The lantern light fell over the shaman's eyes; they were small things, like a normal man's. Wearily, I pointed at his body. "Give me the lantern and take him."

Jake looked like he wanted to vomit, but he knew better than to speak a crossword against the dead man, redskin or not. He picked up the body and something lumbered in the shadows in front of him, the log shattering under its weight. I held the lantern in my hand and could see the glowing eyes.

Jake backed up, cradling the old shaman close and scurrying behind me like I was any more use. The heavy panting followed him. I began the walk back to the stagecoach, back to my horses and my collection. Even though Dead Bear must have been heavy, Jake never once slowed down. Neither did the massive thing that kept to the shadows, claws clicking against the stone.

"The damn hell is that?" Jake whispered.

Might've been a spirit, or a demon, or the soul of a man left face down in the dirt praying curses on all men.

I told Jake the barest truth. "It's just a bear, nothing more." Didn't give him comfort, just britches full of piss and a hurried walk to get out of the valley.

CHAPTER FOUR

PICKED UP SOME chains in Littlecreek
heading up into Kansas. A few days' ride, the
dead shaman had been quiet for all of them.

Jake might have known the faces of the Bad Hand,
but he'd only known where one was heading.
"Maddox aimed to strike it rich in Dakota Territory.
Custer expedition went there last year, and he'd heard
tale of all sorts of boots coming back filled up with
gold. Always said he was going to find the end of the
rainbow up there. He sold his part of the white buffalo
to Lamb, it finally gave him the coin to muster out and
head north. Last I heard, he had signed up with some
buffalo hunters who were heading up into Missouri."

Jake laughed at that. I had sat quietly, thinking it
over before turning north, only stopping in our
journey to have the smithy work up the metal bonds.
I'd wrapped them around the coffin, ignoring the
deep whispering that was coming from inside. Jake
had watched me the entire time as I made sure each
link crisscrossed over the scarred wood.

"What's the point? He's dead, right?"

That elicited a chuckle. He'd been riding with me
for only a few days and he was already learning to ask

the right questions. I'd learned a lot of things in my time, but one of the earliest was in a one-room schoolhouse where I'd asked questions about God when she'd read from an old and worn Bible. Sometimes the right questions didn't lead to fulfilling answers.

"Ever seen a corpse, days old, fall out of a box? I have and it ain't an experience I'm eager to repeat."

The coffin lid bounced and something groaned inside. I glanced back at my companion, but it looked like he hadn't heard anything. Best thing for him; he'd sleep better at night when this was all over.

Asked around Littlecreek while Jake spent the last of my coin on fresh supplies. It was a small settlement, as these things went; the whole of it probably lived and died on the presence of the railhead, taking cattle all across the country and bringing fresh folks in. The local saloon doubled as a barber and, as I felt the coins in my pocket, I wondered what the going price was on a whiskey and trim. I trusted Jake to handle our grub, but the pup wouldn't know his way around good whiskey if the devil himself offered to teach him. Couldn't match Old Scratch in technique, but I was sure that I could give it my damn best.

The wall outside was covered in old notices for events long since passed and broadsheets for the local element. There were a few bigger names; Jesse and Frank were both featured prominently. I tipped my hat to the poster as I passed, silently wishing for my old friends to keep giving the bastards hell.

The bartender glanced up when I entered. Daytime drinkers didn't look like a rarity; most of them looked fresh off of the railroad with smudges of dirt and sweat. They were mostly Chinamen and Negro gandy dancers. I never had a problem with a man's skin; their souls spent just as well as a white man's.

A few men sat drinking at their tables. Place was prosperous enough to afford a piano player on the regular; he played real spirited in the corner, even singing. I took a moment to appreciate the man's voice before I walked toward the rear of the building, keeping my hat pulled low. I wasn't taking the chance that my name and particulars weren't on one of those broadsheets outside.

The barber had just finished sweeping off some other customer. He fidgeted nervously as I removed my coat, hanging it just below my hat on the stand nearby. His hair was slicked over, nearly jet black, a small cowlick poked up toward the back. He didn't look particularly old, but he wasn't going to have many women running after him; face was too narrow and worn enough that he looked like he had ridden in with the rest of the ranch hands.

I took my place in the chair, locking eyes with my reflection and his in the mirror. The barber took his place behind me. He nearly went into convulsions when he spotted the brand under my eye.

"It-it'll be—" He gulped down a panicked breath before he continued, "fifty cents for a shave and a cut. Twenty-five for just a cut."

I reached out with my hand and dropped the two coins into his quivering hand, trying to ease his mind. "Calm yourself, barber, I'm not aiming to spill any blood today."

The barber seemed to accept my words. I didn't relax, not exactly; a bullet might not have been able to touch me, but a razor could spill liquid rubies faster than I could draw on him.

Anything could set off a jumpy man, learned that more than a time or two, but my curiosity wouldn't be denied. "What's your name, barber?"

The man's hand jumped a bit, drawing a small slit of red close to my jaw. He dabbed at it with a dirty cloth, "Sherman, sir."

"Sherman . . . " I muttered to myself, letting the name flow over my tongue, tasting it. "Tell me your story, Sherman."

The barber's hand twitched as he began to shave. He'd heard the stories, the ones that I'd left behind. He knew that this was going to end one of two ways.

"Please, sir, I didn't mean to. It's stopped bleeding." He gestured at the cut in the mirror. It *had* stopped bleeding; my jaw had a good scruff, free of the long beard I'd been sporting. My hair still needed some tending.

"Tell me your story, Sherman, and don't make me ask again."

The barber laid out that he was from Ohio, a Yankee. He plied his trade for the Union during the war, and he'd never married, never even really taken much interest in ladies around town, said it hadn't really ever occurred to him. He just wanted to make money and practice his craft.

I listened to his story while my Gun whispered. It had been too many days since I'd collected anything other than a story; no souls, no lives, no scalps, no eyes . . . it was building to a fever pitch. It was a hunger, that was the hard truth of it. A hunger for death I'd had ever since my brother and I had been handed our weapons.

John Maddox, the Mick, would be feeling it soon.

It was like looking at a stranger when Sherman the barber clipped the last stray hair from my chin. He'd left the scruff and slicked my hair back so it was neat and shiny. Could've passed perfectly in high Yankee society if I'd the mind to do so.

I stood up from the chair and Sherman whisked the apron from me. I saw the dark locks that had been trying to find purchase fall to the floor in tangles of black. He stood nervously, unsure of what I meant to do. It was the reaction of most men when they knew who I was.

I reached into my coat pocket and pulled out a silver pocket watch I had taken from the body of a ranch hand in Texas. It was worth a hundred times what the price of this trim had been.

"For the story," I said simply, letting it drop into his trembling hand and tipping my hat. I walked to the bar, leaving the man to sweep hair with a new story and a valuable piece in his pocket.

I ordered a double, best stuff in the house, and drifted over to the piano man, placing coins atop the instrument. "Anything but Yankee music."

The piano man accepted it gratefully, cracking his knuckles and beginning to play something somber, sad; made me think of lost causes and dead men.

"Ever think about turning back?"

I was struck out of my drink, my hand immediately jumping to my hip, but the Gun wasn't speaking. I looked at the grip like it was growing snakes. The piano man stared with piercing green eyes, his black vest and white undershirt fastidious and tidy. Didn't look like he had ever spent a day in the dirt.

"Wouldn't do you much good, Salem Covington, but I'm not here to drag you to a noose man or a judge. I'm just here to play music."

I paused for a moment, mulling my options. The man's wrinkles deepened in concentration as he started playing again. "No, don't expect it would do me any good. Got a name or am I just supposed to listen to the music?"

The music man chuckled, shrugging his shoulders. "Does it matter what my father named me? It's just another name for you. Don't think I want to be offering it for your collection."

He knew who I was, knew my habits. I had my theories on why that might be, but of course I could be wrong. Sometimes a man is just a man and sometimes they just knew the stories that floated across the prairie.

"You never answered my question. Ever thought about turning back? Giving up everything and following some other way?"

I'd thought about it, more than a night or two. Sometimes I wished that my brother and I had just wanted to be regular johns instead of what we had become. What sides we'd ended up on. That's the thing about trades and deals; you always think you're getting the better end of it until you realize that you weren't the first sucker that the devil had lined up and knocked down.

The piano man's song had transformed, turned

into an old-time gospel. I wondered if my brother could hear it down in Hell.

I could tell the truth, but I didn't want to give the stranger the satisfaction. "Don't think about it at all, truth be told. Virgil and I knew what we were bargaining for. I've got a ways to go, but I think I'll get there yet."

The piano man smiled a knowing smile. It ground my nerves and set my temper burning, even if he hadn't spoken. "What's so funny?" I asked.

The piano man's fingers flowed over the keys, his old eyes closed and listening to the melody. "Lies are a lot like a wrong note, Mister Covington; they just don't ring right in the grand flow of things. You're a man who is weary, a man who has collected a lot, but if you think that the end of your trail ends in anything but rope, then you're deluding yourself . . . No matter how many things you collect." He chuckled to himself. I swore that I could feel the coarse knots of a rope around my neck. "Just my perspective on things. Might still be time for you, though, if you go about changing your ways; choose the Bible over the Gun."

I frowned, my temper raging, and I pulled the Gun, pushing the barrel under the man's chin. "You believe, Piano Man?"

The man's eyes never widened, he didn't even look afraid. He just sat with the same damn expression of knowing and continued to play. "I believe you're going to put a whole lot more into the ground before you swing, Salem Covington."

Would have threatened him for his name, tortured him for details, if not for the boy bursting through the door and hollering to high heaven. "Marshall done caught a deserter! They're going to hang him!"

I knew in my heart that he was talking about Jake, and despite the Gun's near shouting in my head, I put it back into the holster.

The Piano Man looked at my hand and at the stream of men pouring out of the Saloon. That knowing smile turned into a weary shrug. "Might want to look to that, Mister Covington. I'm just going to keep playing."

Reluctantly, I left him there. Only turned around to look once, but my theory about who he could be must have been wrong after all; he was still there playing when I looked.

CHAPTER FIVE

FOLLOWED THE flow of the crowd. The gallows were on the edge of town, where the road turned south to head back into Indian Territory. They were already worked into a frenzy. It looked like a docket of three today, and Jake was just an addition. I saw an Indian, a man who looked like he was about to piss himself in fear, Jake, and a woman dressed in deep maroon.

A man in a deep mahogany vest stood next to them. I could see the marshal star pinned to his chest. He had muttonchops of grey and a sharp goatee that made him look like some tent congregation's idea of the devil.

Four cavalrymen stood around the gallows; looked like a Yankee patrol that had just happened on Jake. Must've been from Fort Sill to recognize him.

A group of deputies were on the scaffold, three that I could count.

All of them would be dead in a few moments if things went south.

There was a good fort's worth of townspeople lingering around, eager to watch a few deaths to take their minds off the roughness of living. The man with the sharp chin stepped forward, his maroon coat billowing in the wind as he held up two black-gloved hands for silence. "You all know me, been the law around these parts long enough; brought peace where I could after the war and my part in it." He spoke with a drawl. Wasn't a Yankee. I didn't recognize him, so he had more than likely come up after the war was over.

"You folks bled around here for too long, suffered and lost to vermin like these, and that's why we are here today, to let folks all over this territory know that we believe in justice."

The crowd erupted into cheers. I stayed silent and looked at the faces of the others destined to hang. I wondered at their names and stories, whether they had anything that I would find useful in my collection.

My companion didn't look afraid, wasn't jumping in his boots or sobbing with slumped shoulders. Truthfully, he looked stunned by it all; more like he was wondering how he had come to this in a few days' time.

He caught my eye and I gave him a slight nod of my head. The stupor wore off of him and his face became grave. He knew that I would spill blood before that rope tightened around his neck.

The Marshal continued his speech. "The following are condemned to death by hanging, charges as follows: Tall Sky: rustling cattle and murder. Elmer Holcomb: larceny, assault, and murder. Jacob Howe: desertion and murder. Ruby Holloway: murder."

The crowd cheered and hurled abuse at them. I closed my eyes and listened to the cries of "fucking redskin", "liar", "whore", "thief", "coward", "scum", and all the rest of the names and epithets that could be used to shame condemned men and women.

The woman, Ruby, began to holler, her dark hair swirling around her as she strained against the rope. "BASTARD PULLED A KNIFE ON ME! I'M INNOCENT! I WAS JUST LOOKING OUT FOR MY OWN—" The marshal walked down the scaffolding and backhanded the woman. It left an ugly red mark on her cheek and she quieted immediately.

The marshal was panting; apparently hitting women took a lot of out him. I saw him raise his paper full of charges to the air. "You've been found guilty, Miss Holloway. You'll have time to say your piece, but until then keep your dirty mouth shut."

Judging by the abuse being hurled towards her, I guessed she'd worked late hours at the saloon.

I could have waited for him to give them their piece, let them say their final words, but the Piano Man's words had been driven under my skin like a railroad spike and my quarry was getting further away by the minute. The Gun felt good in my hand as I eased it out of its holster. It spoke to me, made the same promises it always did, stroked my mind like a whore stroked my pecker. I wanted to fire and draw death rattles then and there, but I'd always been a man who offered folks chances. Even if I knew they wouldn't take them.

I shoved through the crowd until I was at the front, then I held my Gun aloft and fired in the air. A few people behind me screamed and ran back a few paces. The deputies and cavalrymen all drew iron and pointed in my direction. Things would get bloody if they were slippery with those fingers; there were an awful lot of folks behind me.

"Son, I don't know what kind of condition you

have, but my deputies are going to have to escort you to the jailhouse. You don't know how close you came—"

I lifted the brim of my hat, cutting the marshal off completely when he saw the brand under my eye.

"Holy shit, lucky day in my jurisdiction. All the stories I'd heard about you, Mr. Covington, spoke like you were the devil, not a simple-minded fool."

Pointing one finger at Jake, I made my offer. "I just want him. Hand him over and you can live. Hang the rest. I've got business north of here and he knows the man I'm seeking."

Silence reigned for a moment, blink of an eye really, and like the shadow of a passing bird, it was over just as quick. They started laughing, it was a mocking laugh, an incredulous laugh. I didn't waste any time in killing the nearest man.

The back of his throat exploded as my Gun roared. The bullet tore through the skin and shattered his spine. He dropped like a bag of flour, thudding hard against the ground and struggling to move his limbs as he drowned in his blood, eyes darting around the gallows.

I'd killed another before they began shooting, one of the cavalrymen. He took two shots to the chest, ugly holes opening up in his pristine uniform. The blood came running out as he fell back, dead before he hit the ground.

Marshal was quicker on the draw than the rest. He fired, but the bullet skimmed my shoulder and hit a man in the leg while he was trying to run. He went down screaming.

I was going to save that man for last, collect his

story while I was at it. Maybe his coat too. Let him shoot at me for all his gun could hold; I couldn't be killed by it.

One deputy ran, a smart man, but the other was brave and met his end when my bullet punched right into his temple, sending a splattering of blood and skull fragments across the condemned man, Edgar Holcomb, who went to caterwauling like a newborn babe.

One of the cavalrymen rushed from beneath the scaffolding. I barely had time to register him there, before his rifle barked and a woman running behind me screamed as the bullet found her back. Then he was on me and we were rolling in the dirt. He was big; I could smell whiskey on his breath. In another life, he would have roared at the Lord's people and waited for a shepherd boy to come and lay him low. But there weren't any shepherd boys here today, just me, and I could do better than slings and stones.

I wrestled my arm out from under the man. He hit hard, but my Gun bit harder. I felt a vibration in his side when I pulled the trigger, the bullet passing through his guts, tearing it up as they went. The man's eyes went wide and I stared into them as deep as I could. I wondered if he realized that he was dead, his juices spilling inside him. He coughed a little, blood bubbling at the corners of his mouth, running down his chin to drip onto my face, then the lights went off and he slumped over me.

I pushed him off of me, angling him so that the remaining two cavalrymen and the marshal wouldn't be able to send a few bullets to sully my vest or coat any more than the blood soaking from the dead man already was. The man's body spasmed with each bullet that peppered him. I reached around the dead meat and squeezed off two more shots that shattered the kneecap of one of the cavalrymen and sent the other to the Promised Land as his eye exploded, bits of blood and jelly running down his cheek as he fell to his knees and collapsed into the grass.

"Son of a bitch! SON OF A BITCH!" The marshal was hollering full tilt. I dropped the dead goliath, and stood with my arms outstretched, mocking him. He fired, missed, fired again, missed again, each bullet found its way into the ground behind me, beside me, flew off into the air. I smiled when his gun ran dry, his finger futilely pulling the trigger, his eyes darting around like a rat in a trap trying to find a path that didn't end in me killing him.

In the end he started yelling, defiant, just like most did when they were facing the end. "You can't do this, Covington! I'm the law around here! I'm important; posse will hunt you to the ends of the state to see you swing if you kill me!"

I didn't answer him; the man didn't deserve an answer. I just watched him pace up and down the scaffolding, my Gun trained on him the entire time.

"You're a relic, the war's over! Been over for near ten years. We lost. I changed, moved on, and became a respectable man, unlike you. You're a savage and will die like one." His hair had come undone, slicked down bits of grey were now strung out with sweat, the sharp chin goatee dripping with his spittle.

I supposed he wondered when I was going to shoot him. If he'd learned how to count he would know that I had used all six shots. I'd be able to kill him, that much was certain, but not before he pulled the lever and sent my companion swinging.

Jake met my eyes and something passed between us, an unspoken agreement. The marshal walked back in front of my companion as Jake strained against the noose.

The condemned man covered in blood, Edgar Holcomb, began to shout when he realized what was happening. "Marshal! Marshal!" The man's guttural voice rang out. The Marshal turned only in time to see Jake's boot kicking into his gut.

The man made a sucking sound, trying to draw breath as he lost his balance, tumbling off like he was a feather floating on the wind and thudding into the dirt. I had to give this Marshal his due; he came to his feet quick, only to find my knife under his throat.

The Marshal swallowed, staring up into the blue sky as I quietly asked him the pertinent question. "You know who I am. Now tell me, what's your name?"

His eyes rotated to meet mine, and he spit, the saliva mixing with the blood of the dead man still staining my skin. They were fearful green eyes; it let me know that he finally believed. "I know the stories about you. I'd rather be damned than give you my name!"

A deep and bitter chuckle escaped my lips and I dragged him toward the scaffolding, listening to the deep and howling agony of the cavalryman with the shattered knee as Jake began to call, trying to get my attention.

I kept my Gun trained on the Marshal's forehead as I cut through the bonds on Jake's hands. My companion slithered out from the rope around his neck like it was burning and went to take the noose off from the woman, Ruby.

"Stop," I commanded coldly. Jake turned, looking stupefied. I wondered how I looked in his eyes, the sun burning through my orbs as the brand under my eye shined bright. "Not until I'm done. A life for a life. You wait and then I'll let you make your decision."

Jake didn't get my meaning, but he would.

I holstered the Gun, keeping the knife to the Marshal's throat, backing him up to the noose. He began to stammer, speaking platitudes and promises that held no meaning for me. "Mr. Howe, bind his hands." The Marshal's platitudes became threats, once again imploring me to consider his importance, who he was, who he had been.

When my companion was through, he stepped back. The Marshal began to work on our shared allegiance; we had both fought for Dixie, I couldn't kill a fellow veteran.

I had fought for myself, not for Dixie, but I still couldn't abide traitors and sellouts.

It was the condemned Sioux who spoke up. "Save your breath, lawman. There is no deal struck with Sapa Halhata."

The Marshal's eyes darted down to the man whose death sentence he had just read to the cheering crowd. Edgar Holcomb's eyes followed, both men staring at the Sioux man, though only the Marshal had the courage to speak. "What . . . what does that mean?"

I nodded to the Sioux, Tall Sky. He wasn't a member of the People, but he was close enough to know, to understand, and see what was coming. He answered quiet and certain. "It means Black Magpie."

I let my knife trail over the Marshal's cheek. The tip drew a red line across his skin and he winced. I leveled it at his temple, locking my eyes with his. They widened when he realized my plan.

"You won't give me your name. Good thing I don't want it anymore."

Jake would tell me sometime later that he had heard a story of this; that folks in Littlecreek, Kansas had shut their windows and doors, put cotton in their ears, and even sang Grace at the top of their lungs, but it hadn't been enough to shut out the Marshal's wails. Jake told me that children still suffered nightmares as they imagined what was happening on the gallows outside of town.

I didn't have to imagine at all.

The skin peeled easily enough; it always did. The Marshal stamped his feet and screamed, tears running down his face. It was bright red and flowed thick. I saw the yellow bit of his skull and reached with my hand to feel the rubbery texture of his flesh, getting my hands around it in a firm grip and pulling . . .

The Marshal was a tough man, he never passed out as I tugged, each bit of skin ripping off slowly, bloody strings of sinew and hair desperately attempting to keep this man's scalp from being separated.

Edgar Holcomb watched with wide eyes stained with tears, occasionally offering a terrified wail to match the Marshal's own. Tall Sky watched without outburst or sorrow. Jake vomited onto the scaffolding, the whore, Ruby following suit.

I knocked a knuckle against the Marshal's skull. There wasn't much energy left in him now, and with the amount of blood covering me and the gallows, he was a dead man.

Haste was of the essence. I turned to Jake and lifted two of my fingers. "You can have two."

"What?" He could barely find his voice.

I patiently explained it to him. "You were going to live no matter what. This Marshal and the cavalryman, I mean to kill them, but they'll be taking the places of the people they meant to condemn. I don't expect you to understand, but just suffice it to say I pay my debts."

I stalked to the cavalryman. He breathed hard and screamed in panic, futilely trying to fight off my grip as I looked back at Jake. "Pick two, now."

He picked the whore first, delicately removing her noose with a smile. I dragged the cavalryman there and placed the noose around his neck, unbinding the ropes from around the woman's wrists and tying his instead.

The cavalryman told me his name was Matthew, like this would save him now. His story was of no interest to me.

I looked at Jake. The woman had sheltered behind him as if that would save her should I choose anything for her but life. "One more, Mr. Howe."

Jake looked at the other end of the scaffolding with distaste. To save the coward, or the savage? To see the decisions of a man's soul, those are the things that one remembers, the moment you could repeat in stories told in saloons years later.

I waited patiently.

The young man stepped between The Sioux and The Thief, staring into each man's face.

"Please mister, please!" Edgar Holcomb's voice rose to a high keen. The noose shook in the wind, the wood creaking as his boots stomped and jumped. "I'm not ready yet, I'm not ready yet, I'm not ready . . . no!"

Jake had stepped away from him to look at the Sioux. Tall Sky stared at him as my companion stared back. He didn't try to hide the look of loathing that crossed his face, but he did try to hide the look of sympathy, the look of pity. Sometimes a man is a savage, not equal to the shit of a horse in the street.

Jake turned away, wiping his face, and removing the noose from Edgar Holcomb's neck.

I nodded. Sometimes a man was just a man.

Edgar's cries of thanks and gratitude were nearly drowned out by the other cavalryman's pleas for mercy as I dragged him to the rope. When he was settled, I looked at Tall Sky. Mayhaps I owed him something, maybe I didn't. Either way, I promised that I would remember him. The Sioux man nodded, then he began to sing. I wondered if my teacher had been afforded the same death song.

I stopped at the Marshal's limp form on the scaffolding. Dragging him to his feet and placing one of the vacant nooses around his neck. When I stepped back, I slapped the Marshal. It stained my glove with more blood and his eyes revolved around in his head, bouncing around to points in the air like he could see things that I couldn't.

Jake moved Edgar and Ruby off the trap door and I pulled the lever.

There was a drop and three distinct snaps. Tall

Sky died instantly, but I had taken my time when I made the nooses for the cavalryman and the Marshal. I listened to those gurgles and gasps as both men twitched, legs clawing at the air like they'd find somewhere to stand and live.

When that last spasm shot down their spines and there was nothing but the wind and the sound of waiting crows, only then did I turn away. "Let's go, Mr. Howe."

We'd left the stagecoach on the outskirts of town. I knew the trail now and John Maddox waited.

My companion continued to stand on the scaffolding as I descended. Ruby stood next to him while Edgar was curled in a fetal heap, sobbing.

"What about . . . what about her? Or him?"

I didn't turn around; instead I listened to the silence, the blessed silence. It wasn't often that the Gun wasn't whispering murder to me. "They're your lives now, Mr Howe. You traded for them. You do what you will with them."

I took a moment for myself when I reached the bottom of the gallows. I removed my hat for Tall Sky and spit into the dust for the other two with their bulging eyes and swollen tongues.

I thought about John Maddox and the things worse than this I would visit on him.

CHAPTER SIX

"WE'VE PICKED UP the trail, old man. They're following a few buffalo . . . you know there ain't too many of them left."

The coffin lid bounced up and I heard a rumbling groan, like he was frustrated with my words. I shook my head. It was times like these that I wondered what I wanted to say to him, even wondered a little why I was doing this. Virgil and I might have promised ten thousand souls, but there had been nothing owed to my teachers.

"Sorry about the bump, Mr. Covington." She had a soft voice, sweet like morning nectar. I had been wondering how often she'd charmed johns into parting with their coin just for another sweet song from her.

Jake gestured at her, almost panicked, a finger to his mouth. I'd turned an impassive eye on both of them and Ruby Holloway, former lady of the evening, went back to urging Soldier and Maestro onward.

I'd taken the Marshal's horse. His scalp was tied to the saddle and my teacher had been pleased when I had told him the tale. Then he'd begun to rage when I told him of Tall Sky. The chains were sturdy and they held fast. He'd grown silent toward me after that, even if I'd kept him informed of things.

We'd passed the bison skeletons. I was pretty sure Maddox was moving in a wagon train as he headed north; better for protection that way, but slower and easier to track.

It'd been three days since Littlecreek. Couldn't say what had become of Edgar Holcomb, we'd left him where he'd been spared, but Ruby had stuck to Jake like some kind of savior. The woman had barely spoken to me, a fact that I was grateful for. I couldn't remember the last time I'd had traveling companions for this length of time. She'd looked back at me whenever I spoke to my teacher. It gave me comfort to speak to Dead Bear, even if she couldn't understand the way he responded, every bump and groan of the wagon as clear to my ears as wordplay. I reckoned that she thought best not to ask after that, and like Jake, she had lapsed into a silence towards me, only speaking to me when I spoke to her.

But with Jake, she must've been a chatterbox. They whispered like thieves intent on robbing some traveler; fast, joyful, and with wicked grins.

I'd watched them, even when they thought I was riding by myself some ways off. It struck my curiosity; the seeds were there for more and I wondered if Jake would take advantage of it. The senorita in Querido would be devastated if she knew. Jake had described her to me when I'd asked, told me of dark beauty and passion that would have set dust to burning. Catarina, that was her name, and she sang in a little cantina. Mayhaps I'd pay her a visit one day after my business was concluded.

The terrain was mostly flat; a few rises here and there, but with the right equipment you could see miles in every direction. It hadn't been unduly difficult to spot the wagon train, with the bits of white canvas against the blue sky. I lowered my binoculars and listened to the whispers coming from my hip.

The Gun said that Maddox was there. Of course, the weapon was just hungry for blood, it would have whispered anything if it meant I'd be drawing iron.

I held up my hand and heard Ruby bring the stagecoach to a stop. We were just below a rise, the wagon train maybe three miles off over open field. I didn't want some scout with a good eye to spot us before I was ready.

I wasn't keen on slaughtering some folks trying to make lives for themselves; migrants and decent people weren't sinful enough to work toward my debt, and I didn't feel like dealing with the posse that would create. After Littlecreek, I was sure one of those were being rounded up.

"What is it? Is it the wagon train?" Jake had dismounted from the stagecoach and joined me on foot, squinting hard against the sun.

"Wagon train, alright. Can't be sure yet if it's the right one." I dismounted from the Marshal's horse; hadn't bothered to ask for his name when I'd killed his former owner.

I'd known a boy once, name of Tobias, and his horse had wandered out in the pasture and been mauled by a bear in Colorado Territory. He'd gone out to help his friend and had found himself occupying that same bear's stomach. That bear had become clothing that adorned my teacher and I'd been tasked with burying Tobias' digested head. Couldn't rightly say why this horse brought back that memory, but Tobias seemed as good a name as any for a horse.

"We'll set up camp. You and I will go in when it gets dark, draw close and see if Maddox is with them."

Jake nodded and drew back to the stagecoach, reaching up and helping Ruby dismount. Twin puffs of dust came up from the prairie and she smiled at Jake gratefully. "I guess I'll start cooking up something."

"No fires," I said, leading Tobias to a good plot of land and hitching him there. "I don't want them to see smoke before we make our move." I gestured to the stagecoach. "I have supplies inside. Feel free to scrounge and take what you need."

"Sure, Mr. Covington. I'll see what I can make for us." She spoke fast, unsure of where she stood with me, and she didn't keep eye contact for very long.

This was a good thing.

Ruby cinched up her dress, moving back toward the door and reaching for the handle. She wouldn't last if a posse caught up to us or if my teacher found a way past those chains.

"Miss Holloway, you'll find women's clothes more suitable to the wild inside. Take what you will and leave that dress behind you."

The former whore looked at me, her eyes full of questions, probably wondering where I had acquired such things and no doubt better off for not knowing.

"Make sure she doesn't touch anything but the clothing, Mr. Howe. Without the proper protection, you're more than likely to die from doing so."

Ruby opened her mouth and closed it again just

as quick, giving the inside of the stagecoach a worried glance as Jake hurried over and put a reassuring hand against her shoulder, whispering something that was more than likely comfort.

I had other business and watching courtship wasn't a part of it. "Keep a watch, Mr. Howe, and don't let us get caught with our pants down."

The coffin was chained to the back of the stagecoach, where once the illustrious company of Johnson and Rankin Bank and Trust had kept lockboxes of valuables on route to other places: payrolls, dynamite, bank notes, things of value to some. Now it was the bed that my teacher would lay in on his way to whatever boot hill I'd plant him in.

I unhitched the chains that kept the coffin secure, walking around and pushing it to the ground. The lid bounced and something resonant and vast came from inside, displeased that I had disturbed his death rest. Pulling the links tight, I made sure they were secure. The lid could open slightly but only just enough for someone to slip a hand in. Or for my teacher to slip a hand out; one of the things I worried about in the long cold hours of the night when Jake and Ruby slept and I kept my eyes and my mind tuned to the stranger things of the world.

I saw Jake watching, a dangerous curiosity that I hoped to drive from him plastered on his face. Maybe he'd spy on me while I went about my business. It was a natural inclination. If he died from it, there were still ways to get what I wanted.

I looped one of the chain links around my hand and pulled. The coffin was heavy, but only because of the wood, not the body that was inside. It didn't catch dirt as I dragged it, the grass and roots didn't bite into the wood as it passed over them. There was power in these chains and old dead oak that wouldn't be marred by something as plain as earth.

I dragged my teacher far enough from the stagecoach that I was sure that Ruby and Jake would not be eavesdropping, far enough they couldn't see. A decent rock outcrop hung above my head, the scraggly roots of dead trees shooting down through the rock as I dragged my burden underneath into the shadows.

It would suit my purposes; the shadow would hide us from the sun, a necessity when you went about practicing dark things. I left my teacher in the shadow of the rock and went looking for things I would need: kindling, stones for a fire pit, bones if I could find them.

The plains of Kansas were barren, blue sky and clouds looking down on the occasional tree, dried grass, and dusty creek bed. I went to a tree first, gathering loose sticks that had fallen during the dry summer, occasionally stopping to pick up a stone that looked like it would do well for the small fire I would need. A discarded log and stump produced a black widow spider. Any with venom would have done, but I was especially fond of these. Solitary and deadly, a kinship that I could identify with.

I produced a small glass jar from the folds of my satchel, scooping up the angry arachnid and placing it back into the dark leather. Everything else I would need already occupied my satchel, the benefit of travelling far and wide across the nation.

I returned to the overlook, the chained coffin undisturbed. There was movement at my feet, an exodus of the insects that had been sheltering under the rock's shadow, beetles scurrying towards grass, worms wriggling from the soil, uncaring of the hot sun they would most certainly die under. Even a mouse came squeaking from somewhere and vanished into the prairie. None of them wanted to occupy the same ground as my teacher.

I slowly began to build the fire pit, stacking the stones in a circle and adding my kindling to the desolate soil. The coffin was on the opposite side from me, a deliberate decision.

"I would sure appreciate your help with this," I said, folding my coat and placing it aside, my vest and shirt following suit until I knelt bare-chested before the coffin.

My teacher didn't answer, the coffin never moving. I wondered if he had let go of his rage, moved on to the next world. Supposed it didn't matter in the end. If he truly graced the other side, then he could have these men's souls when I sent them there.

I struck a match against my boot, placing the stick into the kindling and sitting on my haunches to watch the flames. The dry sticks caught quickly and I watched the orange light and slight bits of smoke begin to rise. I would have to be quick, lest this grow out of control and give away our position.

I retrieved the wooden mortar and pestle from my satchel, hand carved years ago from a Chinook totem in the Northwest. Mushrooms I had collected from the edges of the Mississippi River went inside and I slowly began to grind them up until there was nothing but a wet paste.

Nature gives men a lot to fall back on, but to see

behind the veil, and interact with the secret things of life, sometimes you need to fall forward. I drank the paste, letting the rubber texture and disgusting sourness of the fungus stick between my teeth and gums. It was only then that I began to whisper the words that I had been taught. It was old magic, secret rites that had been told to few, lest they lose their power.

I could feel my stomach beginning to turn into knots as the spell went to work on me, nausea gripping tight. My knife was in my hand and I carved one line into my left palm, letting the thick and running blood drip into the fire and steam. My vision began to blur, and it was at that time that the coffin across from me rumbled, the chains bouncing and vibrating. I heard a voice out of that dark slit, heavy and low-pitched like a roar. It matched the words I was mumbling as I reached with one hand toward the last part I needed.

The Black Widow struggled against the glass, desperate to run from the black rite I was performing. I unscrewed the lid and reached down into the jar, grabbing gently by the abdomen, immediately feeling two small fangs dig into my flesh. The venom was good; it was what I needed.

I placed it on my stomach and let it bite thrice more. When I felt that third bite, I released it, eight black legs like tiny pinpricks scurrying across my chest and into the dirt.

The blue sky had turned black, but there were not stars. I felt my bones and limbs begin to seize and I fell back onto the ground. My head turned toward the fire and the coffin behind it. The chanting had stopped, and instead Dead Bear sat on the coffin lid, eyes boring into mine.

I stood and, when I looked down, my body still lay wide-eyed and shaking.

It was a dangerous working and I didn't have long. That was the risk of something like this; you'd cut the mortal rope short and be driven along spirit winds to dead plains.

Dead Bear's scowl cut me more than any sin, but he knew why I had come to this place. I'd come to see if I could divine my brother's weapon and the hand that now wielded it.

Hard go of it, living under the threat of one bullet in one gun, being carried by someone who—by hell, fate, or just plain circumstance—hated you more than any other.

Last I had seen it was at Marmiton River. I'd tried to retrieve his weapon, a Gun that matched mine, its twin, and the one thing that could put me under the ground. I didn't sleep easy some nights knowing that the old snake's promise still stood:

"Fate and folly will find your weapons drawn to each other, unable to die unless it be by brother trigger."

Virgil and I hadn't thought we'd be drawing on each other; the ignorance and boldness of youth.

Dead Bear pointed a finger out into the dark. I followed his gaze. I couldn't tell what was out there, but I could hear things.

I'd crossed over a time or two. Where I had retrieved Dead Bear's body had been right on the border of the other side. But here, fully in the dark, no iron or blade would protect me.

I took a breath to put the fire in my spurs, and then I left my body behind, hoping that my teacher would still have some affection for me. Anything looking for a free ride wouldn't get past his claws or teeth.

I walked past the tree. It stretched and warped in the dark like a giant who had been living on dirt and old bones, it's pale face and longing mouth stretching desperately for me as I went past.

Things twisted, warped; there were no colors here, just the dark. Something splashed through dirty water. An elk or deer cried somewhere distant and coyotes yipped far off.

There was something like thunder, a few flashes of light, and the ground around me exploded. I fell ass over kettle into the mud and murk as figures charged past me in the dark, screams and battle cries echoing in the gloom. I instinctively reached for my Gun that wasn't there.

Without that weapon, without that protection, I didn't feel powerful anymore, didn't feel like a man possessed. I only felt naked.

Feet charged over me, knocking the fire out of me and pressing my face into the mud. I struggled hard to breathe as I sputtered in the brown water, tasting the dirt and worms crawling through it.

I was in a creek, the past, a place I knew. It wasn't like I remembered; there was no sunlight to see by, just the flickering glow of the fire that I had lit, seeming to burn perpetually behind me.

A man in grey rushed me, yelling at the top of his lungs. His bayonet lunged and I fell back, I heard all of the death cries of a thousand men. Horses neighed in agony as cannonballs punched holes through their innards and shrapnel skewered bone.

The man in grey didn't stop. He came at me again, blade attempting to spear my guts. My hand reached out into the water and I felt something familiar . . .

It was a Gun, same as mine, but for the symbol on its hilt. A long time had passed since I had seen that Gun, but it whispered in my head just the same. I fired. The man in grey fell dead and I scrambled to retreat.

Time blurred and I was somewhere else, a river, and another place I knew by heart.

This was where it had been decided.

I stood in the river, Gun in hand and whispering. I was sure of myself, unlike my brother; there was nothing in him but selfishness and rot. He'd let Leraje's promises of power tempt and destroy. He'd perverted every bit of knowledge he'd ever learned.

He came at me from the Confederate lines; I could have spotted him out of any number of men. He strode into the river, his uniform adorned in all manner of things, trinkets from the dead.

I'd heard tell of what the soldiers called him: the Black Magpie. But I knew he was just a man. A man just as scared of the Gun I held as I was of the one he was gripping tight.

"Give up, Salem! War's lost, you boys just don't know it yet!"

My brother was nothing but a dark specter, like something that had been called straight up from hell.

His eyes were like an animal's, light reflecting off of them like he was a beast in the dark.

I fired.

I gasped and reeled back, stumbling in the water. The daylight and figures disappeared and were replaced with nothing but the flickering fire.

Hard to tell here, sometimes you saw things through your own eyes and sometimes you were seeing them through your kin's. I'd been sucked in by my brother's memories and only seeing that dark shadow of myself from ten years ago had snapped me back to myself.

I wasn't Virgil, I was Salem Covington. I was alive, he wasn't. His Gun, where was it now?

The water splashed around me. I intended to follow the river as long as I could; it most certainly had taken the Gun when my brother had fallen.

I panted hard, my heart beating fast in my chest, limbs numb. I knew I was running out of time, but that desire to know stayed with me like a horsefly. I was close and I could feel it.

The stream ended and I walked out of the river onto mud and a field of decimated stumps. A misshapen moon hung in the air and spilled sickly light in front of me.

A man crouched naked and pale against the mud. He was on top of something, and in his hand I saw the distinct pearl handle bearing the same symbol as the one on my cheek. He brought it down and something cracked. Mist steamed out from under him and I smelled blood.

The naked man bent over and I drew closer. I recognized the odds and ends of what had once been a body, now beaten and mauled beyond recognition. A pile of meat steamed in the cold air, the stranger stroking it almost lovingly.

My boot snapped a twig and the pale figure rolled around on his haunches and aimed the Gun. It fired and I was sent tumbling back.

The last thing I saw was the naked man's face, those eyes that were like pinpricks of night, a mouth with snake teeth, and a blood-smeared smile.

"MR. COVINGTON! MR. COVINGTON!"

I heard Jake's voice. My limbs felt like someone was pressing a branding iron into them.

"SALEM!"

My eyes flew open and I saw Jake leaning close, Ruby behind him, her hand covering her mouth.

I desperately felt for the Gun and breathed deep when I found it sitting where I had left it. It hurt to turn my head. Cold sweat covered me, my tongue felt swollen, and deep red sores were beginning to form where I'd let the spider work its craft. Wasn't afraid to admit that I was hurting; felt like I'd been kicked by a horse and cut on by a sawbones.

Wearily, I struggled to sit up. I felt Jake's arms reach under me. Didn't vomit until I was fully upright. The contents of my stomach splattered into the dead fire pit, just a bit of smoldering coals and sticks now. The coffin across from me was still.

Ruby stepped around Jake and looked at the

remains of my retching. "Mr. Covington, did you eat mushrooms?"

I waved her off weakly. I didn't have time to debate the finer points of spell craft.

"You go to some bad places, eating these. I entertained a man once who had bought a few from some Comancheros. Sent him straight to the doc; died from it too." Ruby's eyes were clouded over, remembering her former line of work. I wondered if that had been the man that she had been condemned to hang for.

"I'm fine," I managed to croak out, coughing and breathing deep. My journey to the other side had taken longer than I thought; the sun was beginning to set and had painted huge swaths of purple and orange across the sky. The evening star peaked through a few grey wisps of cloud. The dark of night would be here soon.

I had sworn an oath that I wouldn't wait to fulfill.

"Read—ready the horses," I coughed.

Jake and Ruby looked at each other, her emerald eyes boring into his as he gritted his teeth. "Salem, think it may be best if we rest for the night and let you recover. Ride out in the—"

I seized the front of his shirt and dragged him close. I smelled of piss, bile, and death. My eyes locked with his and I whispered, "I've walked leagues tonight, all over time and distance. Seen the past I'd rather not repeat." I shoved him away and staggered to my feet, kicking sand at the both of them and drawing the Gun. "Get the horses ready, now!"

Both of them scurried from the overhang, leaving me alone to stare at the distant horizon, with its stars and silent judgment.

THE MAGPIE COFFIN

Maybe I was too hard on them, but I was rattled. Some poor soul had my brother's Gun. Darker inclinations too, if what I'd seen was the truth of the matter. I couldn't get rid of that biting at the edge of my mind, the one that told me I'd see that Gun again soon.

Until then, I donned my accouterment, like those tales of knights when I was a boy, except I wasn't there to defend some kingdom or rescue a princess.

I had come to burn the fucking world down.

CHAPTER SEVEN

THE SUNLIGHT HAD disappeared leaving a moonless night. Good. The business I had with John Maddox wouldn't be fit for anything but the black, the constellations in the heavens eager to bear witness. I tipped my hat to the three stars in the belt of the hunter; it would watch over my work.

Jake rode with me. He'd been hesitant to leave the whore behind, but he had not stirred a fuss or argument to dissuade me. He knew what tonight would bring and I had no doubt that he didn't wish to be in the way of such a deed.

I brought Maestro to a halt, Jake following suit with Soldier. We were still a half-mile out, but I could see campfires burning in the circled-up wagons, small shadows flitting around them. I watched with the binoculars, but with no light to see by, I could not say if my quarry was among them.

"What do you think? Do you see him?"

I ignored him, dismounting from my horse and beckoning for Jake to follow suit.

"We aren't . . . We aren't going to get closer?" Jake's voice ran like a straight razor up my back; my patience worn thin after my journey to the other side.

"Don't be afraid. I can't be killed by a gun."

Jake grunted as he dismounted from Soldier. "Maybe, but *I* can and I don't think it's a good idea for us to run up on people who are already jumpy."

"Luckily for the two of us, you aren't the one holding the reins. Find some grit and follow me."

Later, I would look back on this as where my weariness began, but for now, I marched with vigor toward the campfires. I moved quietly, Jake following close behind. I'd learned in my time with Quantrill. I supposed the Yankees had taught Jake similar skills as his footfalls barely made a sound.

We stopped some forty yards from the camp. There was laughter and I even heard children.

"These wagon trains have sentries; two guards on lookout, and one of them usually eats his rations around this time." Jake whispered the information in my ear. I nearly smirked; it was information that I knew, but it was an effort that I appreciated.

I handed the binoculars to him, closing my eyes and listening to the conversations. "Look for him, look patiently. I'm going to listen." He gingerly took them from grip.

Then I whispered under my breath, old words to help me focus on what was out there, to sharpen my hearing and mind. There was a woman traveling with her small dog, to marry an associate of her brother. She confided privately with another woman that she did not look forward to the prospect.

There was a boy. He had swished a bamboo stick back and forth all day, driving an old donkey that his father had paid twenty dollars for. He thought his father had been fooled; even now he hit the donkey across the muzzle when his father wasn't looking.

An old man chuckled, shoveling down his stew like he wouldn't live to see the sunrise. He had information on a good claim; he whispered that he'd live out the rest of his days fat and rich.

A man ate quietly as he cleaned his rifle, spitting the concoction onto the ground and whispering that it wasn't like back home. He thought of the gold.

"That's him!" Jake's whisper brought me out of my trance and I looked through the binoculars at the man he indicated. He sat with a few people around the fire wearing a topper on his head, brown pants, and a dirty white shirt. Bright orange muttonchops ran down the side of his face.

Good to see you, John Maddox.

"What're you going to do, kill everyone in there?"

I had a half suspicion that Jake would have tried to open up my guts if I had confirmed his fear, but I simply shook my head. "I'm going to wait. I have a feeling that Mr. Maddox doesn't like the consistency of his meal."

We didn't have to wait long. Maddox stood up and adjusted his hat, grabbing his rifle from the wagon wheel it was leaning against.

My eyes were closed. I sifted through the sound and gabbing from everyone until Maddox was all that I could hear. "Right shite! Don't know how you Yanks stand it; I need proper meat." John Maddox, who his friends had called 'the Mick', had a thick accent, a holdover from his motherland. I wondered if he sometimes heard it slipping away and spent an afternoon practicing the cadence that his brother immigrants still had fresh off the ships out east. I suspected he did.

"Meat's a little lean, Maddox. Buffalo ain't around like they used to be, thanks to Army folk like yourself." It was an older man who sat at the fire with him, looked like a trapper or maybe a scout, probably hired by whatever company was funding this venture north.

"Whatever horse you used for this shite wouldn't even be appealing to starving flies. I ate better than this chasing Comanche savages through hell and high water."

He loaded a bullet into the rifle, a repeater by the look of it. "Saw bison signs west of here. Any of you think you can muster some feckin' nerve, we'll bring one back."

"Nerve, we got. Smarts, too. It's an ocean out there and we get far enough, we won't be finding our way back." The old trapper spoke truly. More than one settler had starved walking across the grass ocean.

The Mick didn't seem to listen. He looked around at the other members surrounding his campfire. Even if I wasn't close enough to see the dominos falling, I'd seen it play out so many times that I could see every card in his hand. The looks of accusation, challenging their manhood, arguing that their food was going bad and they'd have to stop and hunt eventually . . .

There had been many conversations like that around campfires as rain poured and you huddled close under your blankets trying not to catch pneumonia, tuberculosis, or a bullet to the head.

We'd fed ourselves during those times. If the Mick was so sure of his bison sighting, he would go after it.

West . . . he'd seen it west.

"Let's go," I whispered, drawing back and letting the darkness take us. It wasn't until were a good quarter mile away that I straightened my back and hurried towards the horses.

Soldier and Maestro were where we had left them, eating grass and uncaring about the events unfolding. I handed Soldier's reins to Jake; he'd always been the slower of the pair and I needed speed tonight. "Take Soldier back to camp and wait for me."

Jake looked worried. He ground his teeth together, stroking his chin with one hand and shaking his head. "No, no, I'm coming with you. You're going to need my help."

An effort that I appreciated, but was foolish, nonetheless. "I don't need the help. You've identified him for me and I can wrestle the whereabouts of the rest from him. Besides, your whore might be lonely."

I expected that to be the end of the matter, but Jake was like a dog gnawing at a bone. "She's not my whore; I've only got eyes for Catarina. It was the decent thing not to let her swing. Just like it's the decent thing to go with you, save the life of whatever poor soul is with Maddox."

The saddle was packed with what I needed. I mounted Maestro and sat comfortably in the saddle, looking down at Jake and wondering where this backbone had been when I'd killed his partner back at Ft. Sill. Maybe he thought there was familiarity now, that routine and time had created camaraderie.

He'd forgotten who I was.

The Gun was in my hand and I felt bone and metal collide when I hit him across the face. Jake fell to the ground. The impact had drawn blood, giving him a cut above his left eyebrow. He looked up at me with shock, pain as well, and the question that he didn't voice.

I wondered how I must have seemed through that red curtain. A dark hole in the world riding a horse. "Listen carefully, Mr. Howe. We ain't friends and we ain't partners. When I speak and tell you to do something, just remember . . . " I leaned forward. "It isn't a request. Now get up, go back to camp, and wait for my return."

Jake stared at me and I could see the hate behind that smattering of blood. He spit onto the ground and then stood up on unsure feet. He departed on Soldier without another word.

I watched until the darkness swallowed him, then I rested easy on Maestro, watching for Maddox's departure.

CHAPTER EIGHT

TWO MEN FOLLOWED John Maddox from the camp. There were three horses, a lantern held by the one in the rear. The Mick stopped every now and again, looking at the trail for any sign of bison.

I whispered to the winds, old incantations to bring whatever bison were out there onto our path. Maestro was breathing heavily. I rubbed his neck, letting the horse know that he was doing well, his hoof beats fast but silent in our pursuit.

It came suddenly, that sonorous grunting. I saw Maddox hold up his hand, dismounting from his horse and gesturing for his companions to follow him. They hoisted their rifles and trailed behind him.

It wouldn't be long. I reckoned that I was like an owl, letting the mice and vermin go about their business before my hunger demanded that I take them.

A gunshot rang out and there was a surprised roar of pain. Hoof beats ran in all directions to escape death, then silence.

It was time.

I left Maestro there, making sure I had what I needed before I set out.

"Meat, meat for days!" One of the men who had followed Maddox howled with laughter. I was just over a small rise, watching them as they cut meat out of the carcass. I could smell the sweet scent of blood.

Maddox rested easy on the dead animal's back and watched as his two companions did the work for him.

"Excellent shot, Mr. Maddox. Took it down with one shot you did! Where'd you learn to shoot like that?" It looked like a father and son, skinny things, could practically see their bones from where I stood. Drivers more than likely, hired by the settlers to get their cattle and luggage from Ft. Smith to Dakota Territory.

"Spent a few years in the army, young Thomas. Was a bogger myself until I learned how to kill. Keep an ear toward your Pa there and you'll be wielding weapons just fine. Any old mog can learn how to shoot."

I could discern ancient spells from petroglyphs left on the side of rocks, but the Mick spoke in ways that I didn't understand. The Gun whispered that it wasn't important; just kill him.

"You'll want to keep a sharp lookout, Floyd. I just finished making war on the Comanche, now I hear more redskins and savages are making trouble where we're going. Young Thomas there is going to need to learn his weapons, or he'll end up arse to ground missing his head. I've seen it happen more tha—"

The gunshot rang out and John Maddox's kneecap

exploded. The blood gushed across the stained hide of the dead bison as he fell back, caterwauling like a rabbit on the bad end of a coyote's teeth.

The man, Floyd, and his son, Thomas, both looked around. I heard Floyd scream to his son to get behind him when he saw me.

I grinned broadly. The Gun sang and I fired a bullet straight for Floyd's heart. He stared down for a moment, the hole leaking out bright red. He coughed once, looking at his son in confusion.

I wasn't more than a horse length away now. Thomas sputtered out fresh tears that splattered into the dust as his father fell over, still grasping for his rifle to try to protect his boy.

Something in my heart twisted, but the Gun drowned it out. A bullet came for every man and Floyd would have defended my enemy. I removed the problem before it could become one.

Maddox howled curses and screams from behind the bison. Thomas glanced from me to the Mick between his intermittent sobs. Then he looked at his father's rifle.

"Wouldn't do that, boy," I said it simply. He looked up at me with all the hatred that he had a right to send my way. "Wouldn't do you any good and I'm not for killing children."

The boy screamed and reached for the rifle, but my Gun removed two of his fingers before he could grab it. The kid flopped over on the ground, looking like a near mirror image of his father but for the worm-like writhing.

I cocked my head, looking at the stumps of his left trigger and middle fingers. Little bits of bone poked out like fingernails. His hand was drenched in twin streams of dark blood. He breathed heavy and clutched his maimed paw tight, damning God and me in turn.

I reached down and grasped the boy's shirt tight, bringing him up to my level, and staring him deep in the eyes. "Mark me well. You have a Mama, right? Waiting on you to bring meat back to camp? Proud of you?"

Thomas stared wide-eyed, pain forgotten. I could see the wheels in his head turning, wondering how I knew what his mother had been saying to him before he left camp.

"Leave. Get on your horse and go. Say it was a wolf, or bear; doesn't rightly matter as long as you don't come back here or speak of these things."

I gestured with the Gun at his dead father. "I'll give him a proper burial, you have my word on that, but if you come back to this place, I won't give the same to you or your mother when I'm finished with you both . . . " I let the threat hang in the air, watching as his eyes tracked over mine, memorizing my face. Wasn't going to be too hard to forget; I had no doubt that he was going to be carrying my face for the rest of his life.

"Now go on." I dropped him in time for John Maddox to come stumbling around the bison, hopping on one foot like he was a bird looking for something to eat. He had his rifle raised, but it didn't do him much good. His other kneecap exploded when I fired, his shot going wild. It was like sweet music when I heard that high-pitched screaming.

Leaving Thomas on the ground, I walked to

Maddox and kicked his rifle away from him. I crouched down and reached out for the Mick's chin, lifted it slightly, and saw the anger and pain drain away from his face when he saw the brand under my eye.

"Hello, John," I grinned. "Been looking for you." I twirled my Gun and hit him over the head, knocking him unconscious and silencing his screams. He was bleeding from those shredded holes in his legs; I'd have to work fast before he bled out.

I heard crunching dust and glanced back to see Thomas heading to his horse. He walked in a sideways stumble, cradling his hand tight. His eyes were on me the entire time.

"How old are you, Thomas?" I called.

The boy was at his horse. He hesitated a moment before answering, "Thirteen, sir."

"Remember our agreement, Thomas. Don't speak of the things here and don't come back." I said it jovially, couldn't help it really; excitement always flooded my senses when I caught up with the person I was after.

"I remember, sir." He climbed onto his horse, wincing a bit, but then he called out once more to me. "I'm going to find you one day, mister. After I get Ma taken care of, I'm going to kill you." He spurred the horse and dust kicked up into the air as he vanished into the night.

I chuckled a bit to myself, looking back down at John Maddox. "I'll look forward to that day, kid."

The dawn was coming. I'd done my best to stop the bleeding. Easy enough on the one leg, but my shot had been true and the bullet was still in his other leg. I supposed that I didn't need to remove it, but I was eager for Maddox to arise and smell the ashes.

Maddox's hands were tied together with the bits of rope I had brought. The hole in his leg was dark, clotted. Bits of shredded meat hung across the wound and a few slivers of bone.

I reached down with my thumb and trigger finger. The wound didn't seem big enough to occupy both digits, but then again, I was willing to give it the old devil's try. It felt soft inside, like pomade or gelatin. I imagined that my fingers were like worms digging tunnels underground and it didn't take long for me to touch something hard.

Maddox came awake when I stretched my fingers around the bullet. There were fresh tears and a soft wail as he thrashed back and forth on the ground like a fat caterpillar trying to inch its way across a leaf.

"Hush now, it's out." My hand was covered in his lifeblood, the tiny bullet held between my hands. I flashed it before his eyes; his red muttonchops caked with mud.

"Feck you, you feckin' bastard. I'll kill you, do you hear me? I'll kill—"

I fired once into the ground and then stuck the barrel against the now bleeding wound. The skin sizzled and I smelled that sweet scent of burning flesh. Maddox screamed loud and long, his screams and the sizzling from his cooking flesh mingling. A dark stain spread across his pants and his body shuddered and twitched before he fell back into the black.

Just as well, I needed him in a better position before I started to pry my answers out of him. There was rock nearby, a grey thing just big enough for me to lay his hands across. It was like it had been left there just for me.

I tapped him across the head, watching his eyes roll around before they blinked wearily. "Welcome back, Mr. Maddox. I have a few questions for you."

"You—" He coughed a bit and tried to sit up, but I placed a hand against his chest and slowly shook my head. "You are the one, the one that old redskin spoke about: the Black Magpie. He ran his gob about you before Sergeant Craft worked on him."

I listened to him speak. I wondered if he knew they were going to be his last words.

"You've right fanged me. I think you mean to make it more permanent, yeah?" He was trying to joke, make light of it, maybe appeal to whatever better nature he thought that I possessed. "Listen, I know you think I've wronged you, but I've got a good line on a claim; gold. Neither of us will have to work by the gun anymore, yeah? You fix me up and take me to Dakota Territory and I'll split it with you, real civil like!" He babbled quickly like he was trying to sell me on an old nag that would fall over dead by sunrise.

It was something that I didn't have time for.

"John Maddox, whereabouts are Sergeant Earnest Craft, the Weber Brothers, and Captain Lamb?"

The Mick seemed to shudder and raised his hands towards me, palms out and flat. "Please, Mr. Covington, I'm not ready yet. I didn't touch your savage, I just found him. I'm just trying to make my way!" A fresh round of tears erupted from him and he balled himself tight, his hands clutching at my boots as he sobbed at a fresh wave of pain.

"Again, Mr. Maddox, where are these men?"

The Mick cursed and writhed under my boot. I let him struggle a bit before I reached down with my free hand and yanked one of his fingers to the right. I heard the sweet snap and the following scream. Sobbing came, and I waited until he was finished.

"Their whereabouts, Mr. Maddox?"

Maddox nodded over and over, holding his bound hands with the finger hideously bent out in front of him like it would save him from my anger. "Alright, alright! I don't know where the two gal-sneakers or Captain Lamb are! But Sergeant Craft, he was going to meet me in Deadwood. Damn loony is mad as hops about killing redskins."

An idea seemed to strike him and he smiled broadly showing missing teeth. His eyes were jumping with light. "I never liked him all that much, never liked any of them. Always looking down on a proper Irishman, you know. I'll find him for you, point him out!"

The Weber brothers and August Lamb were still in the wind, but Earnest Craft, practitioner of torture was in Deadwood. I wondered if he would wake this morning in a cold sweat, a nightmare that he couldn't quite remember on his mind.

"Good deal, yeah? I'll even share some of the gold with you. I'm going to need a sawbones after this; you really did—"

I retrieved the hammer I had brought with me, easing it out of my satchel and holstering my gun. John Maddox caught the gleam of metal and his eyes widened. He started shaking his head. "NO, NO, NO! I TOLD YOU, YOU BASTARD! I TOLD YOU WHAT YOU WAN—"

I wrenched his hands back onto the rock and gave him a polite nod. "Thank you very much for the information, but I never said that I was going to spare you."

He screamed incoherently, then he screamed in pain. My hammer fell on the delicate bones in his right hand. I kept pounding away until they were powder under the skin, deep black spreading under his flesh. I went to work on his fingers next, making sure each one was a mangled and unusable wreck.

He'd fallen back into the black when I started work on his second hand. I dragged him over to the bison carcass, wondering if I had brought enough to finish the job. With both hands, I pulled at the flaps of fur and muscle that had been cut through to get at the meat. It was mangled, but it would do just fine.

When I bound the Mick's hands and feet behind him, it brought him back from whatever void his mind had been peacefully resting in. "Welcome back," I said in response to the screaming.

With bloodshot and weary eyes, John Maddox looked up at me, his lips quivering and his mouth pale. "Just kill me, please. You've taken the egg out of me, just no more pain . . . " He paused and let his head droop into the dirt, barely whispering over and over again, "No more pain."

I squatted down next to him, lifting his chin until he saw my eyes. "No use, Maddox. The pain is just beginning."

I had hollowed out a space inside the carcass,

enough space for me to stick a man of Maddox's size. The carcass had already begun to smell, not that it mattered to Maddox. He hollered and squirmed as I shoved him past the meat and bones.

"Don't do this! DON'T, PLEA—"

The darkness swallowed him and I was left with nothing but the screaming. "Might want to keep it down, there isn't going to be much air," I hollered into the meat. If the man had heard me, it didn't keep him from screaming all the louder.

Then I began to sew up the fur, rebinding the cut Maddox and the two Bradfords had made. I hummed in time to the faint begging. The bison's eyes seemed to look at me gratefully when I was finished. The only way that you could hear Maddox now was if you put your ear against the fur. The bison's side vibrated like a rail when a train was coming.

I walked Maestro into the killing field, balking when he smelled the blood. I patted him on the neck, stroking the old warhorse gently. Couldn't have him go and be spooked when I had a promise to keep.

With a length of rope, I bound Floyd Bradford's feet together and threw the loop across the saddle horn. My eyes flicked over to the bison carcass; occasionally there would be a dull thump, but nothing more.

I walked over and placed a hand against the fur. It was still. I went to chiding myself; should have made it last longer. But then the skin moved, just a little bit, and just barely I could hear a dull scream.

Patting the side of the body I whispered into the sewn together death wound. "Take heart, Maddox, you got off easy. I plan much worse for your compatriots."

I left him there as the burning sun rose, scooping up the top hat that the Mick had worn as I went. I headed for home and my companions.

CHAPTER NINE

THE MID-MORNING SUN was shining bright when I rode up on our camp. Ruby crouched beside the skillet, several pieces of bacon frying up and stoking the fire in my belly.

She'd changed; no fancy dress from the city adorned her now. She'd taken a wide brown cattleman's hat that I'd acquired from a drunken cowboy who hadn't had the good sense to back down, and a yellow shirt overlaid with suspenders from her brown pants.

Jake was sitting next to her, a wide bandage around his head. Didn't look much worse for wear except for his sullen gaze.

They heard the hoof beats, both of them drawing iron, twin pistols pointing at me as I dismounted. Jake's eyes flicked to the body behind the horse. His mouth dropped a bit, but he recovered just as quick.

I wrapped the rope tight around my hand. Maddox's hat was perched precariously on my head, and even now it had the smell of death about it from soaking in Floyd Bradford's blood.

Jake stood up. Ruby put a hand on his arm, shaking her head slightly and whispering something that I couldn't hear from where I stood. The former army scout shook her touch off and approached me.

I drug Floyd's body toward the stagecoach. Undertaker would have a hard job of making the corpse presentable; the prairie had done its work, tearing at the skin and caking the dead man with filth.

"That's not John Maddox," Jake said as he reached me.

I nodded. "Just one of those innocents who didn't realize that today was their last."

Jake licked his lips, opened his mouth like he was about to find his nads and spit at me for my goings on. "Did you at least manage to kill him?"

I grinned tightly. "He isn't dead yet, but I give him a day, maybe two, before that changes."

Jake winced, putting his hand against the bandage and pulling it away for blood.

"How's your head?" I asked.

Jake's hand clenched into a fist. "It's fine, all things considered. Ruby managed to patch me up."

Maybe something passed between us, an understanding of some sort, or maybe Jake planned on trying to kill me when my back was turned. It was something I wondered as he passed, calling behind him. "I'll get Maestro settled. Where are we heading next?"

"Deadwood," I replied, hoisting the rope over my shoulder and dragging the corpse down the hill and toward the small fire that Ruby had cooking. She picked up the small bowl of half-eaten bacon and biscuits for me and made to make a space when I waved a hand to stop her.

"Don't go fretting, Miss Holloway. It's been a hell

of a night and I would be most thankful to indulge in what you've managed to make." She wasn't stupid; working as a woman of the line tended to sharpen a girl's edges when it came to spotting flannel mouths, but slowly, like a rolling drop of water, she sat back down.

I went to working my boots off. Ruby turned her nose up at the stench of my unwashed feet as she passed me the plate of breakfast. My stomach groaned and I greedily tore into it. I had no notion of Ruby's time as a whore, but she made a mighty fine grub-slinger.

I was halfway through a biscuit when Ruby asked, "What was it like?" Her voice was soft, hesitating. No doubt Jake had told her how he'd received his whap to the head.

I greedily ate the other half of my biscuit, only answering her once I had swallowed. "To what are you referring?"

Her eyes flitted to the corpse lying face down in the dirt. I followed her gaze before reason overtook me and I smiled briefly.

"I see. What was it like killing a man? Surprised you want to know, considering you were up on the swinging stoop for the same. Or are you claiming that you didn't kill him?"

An understanding passed between us. She wasn't denying anything of the sort; she'd killed the man who'd gotten rough with her, but she was asking how it had felt to savor it.

"It always feels good, Miss Holloway. Most folks don't deserve it, you see, so you do them quick. But for the truly bad ones, myself included, you want to savor it." I gestured at Floyd's body. "He was a good one, but John Maddox is currently soaking in blood and rot."

Ruby wiped the rest of her food into the fire, standing up and brushing up the bits of ash that had billowed onto her shirt. "I'll have to remember that for the next yack thinks he can pull one over on me."

Jake walked past, leading Maestro to the field where Soldier and Tobias both grazed pleasantly. He nodded at the two of us as he passed, but Ruby's eyes followed him like a hawk watching a mouse.

I chuckled and finished the last of the food on my plate, wiping my mouth with the back of my hand. "You're all sand under that shirt, Miss Holloway. Don't think Mr. Howe has realized that yet."

She shrugged and adjusted her Woolsey. "He's still a bit green. Regular prince charming. Keeps me safe from you, I reckon."

I tapped the pearl handle of the Gun. "Nothing would keep you safe if I had to send you to the bone orchard, but you haven't done anything to make me see that's a good course of action."

The former whore nodded and moved to begin cleaning up our used dishes. I called after her, "Fair warning, Miss Holloway, I need him until these four men are dead. Interfere with that, and my view on courses of action is right to change."

I buried Floyd in the alcove where I had cut up shines in the otherworld. A pile of rocks would keep the coyotes and buzzards from an easy meal, but I just didn't have the strength to do more for him.

A bottle of gut burner was in my hand, the cheap whiskey burning thick as I poured it over the top of the rocks. I muttered a simple prayer for the man, whispered some old incantations and then it was done.

Ruby was leaned up against the coach, hat pulled down over her eyes.

Jake sat behind Dead Bear's coffin.

I stood on the edge of the rise, curious to see what would happen. Jake wasn't a man initiated; he'd spent too much time listening to bible thumpers speaking of powers and dominions, all of them preaching to have no truck with what I peddled.

I felt the brand on my face, traced the image. Preachers and church folk might have had the right idea.

Jake was whispering to the coffin. I couldn't make out what he was saying, but when the coffin lid bumped, he went crawling on his rear away from it.

I chuckled as I stepped up behind him. "Shouldn't be frightened, Mr. Howe. It's just a dead man."

Jake pointed, his eyes like an owl, "He's alive! He knocked! I asked him if he would answer me like he answers you and he knocked!"

I tossed the pebble I had picked up at the wooden box. The small rock thumped off the lid and rolled into the dirt.

Jake looked like a man that wasn't accustomed to having the wool pulled over his eyes. He stood up, his mouth turned into a deep scowl that slowly transformed into a chuckle. "Riding with you, Mr. Covington, has a man liable to lose his mind."

I shrugged my shoulders, picking up Maddox's topper from where I had left it in the dirt. "More likely to lose your life, but I can certainly work on the mind if I have the notion to do so."

The thought seemed to unsettle him; his brows furrowed and I saw his fingers begin to fidget.

Couldn't hurt to let him chew on that for a few hours.

"Best get some shut eye; I want to pull up stakes and kick gravel toward Deadwood when the sun goes down."

Jake nodded and headed toward the coach.

I watched him go before I looked at the coffin, grinning in triumph and sitting down where Jake had just left.

I offered Maddox's hat. "Teacher, one of your killers will soon be dead."

The coffin thumped.

CHAPTER TEN

MY TEACHER WAS quiet for the month or so that we spent on the trail. Deadwood was a long way off, and at times I began to wonder if he had crossed over, but my worry was always stifled by bear sign or the hint of a figure watching us when the shadows from the setting sun were longest. Each time, I made sure that the chains holding the coffin were good and tight, that the lid wouldn't open more than a crack.

Jake had remarked how it didn't smell like a dead man inside. Side effect of Comanche practices, I told him. I wouldn't say he believed me; after a month he'd seen me working my craft more than once, had sometimes seen how it played out. It would make a believer out of most.

Ruby was quite a dough wrangler as things went; she stretched our rations along the trip, which was quite a change from my normal routine of hard coffee and old jerky.

I'd never been to Deadwood and my curiosity was beating fast. I'd roamed, wandered, and collected all over, and I was always excited to go somewhere new. Usually involved less risks to my skin and soul, compared to some of the places I'd walked in the past.

I took in everything as we passed the hills and dead trees on the hillside; it looked like a fire had taken them and left nothing but charred stumps and dead soil. Mud and dirty water ran down the bluffs and men with pans in their hands stood ankle-deep sifting through the muck.

I'd seen gold fever before; it seized men, made them like beasts hoping for reprieve from this life. They looked up as our coach came past, and in their eyes, I saw no joy or gold. Just toil and mud.

Deadwood wasn't much to speak of, typical mining town with hastily set up tents. Wasn't surprised to see a few wooden structures; they went up quick where men flocked. I saw a gospel mill, general store, a saloon that doubled as a hog ranch, whores hanging out on the railing and calling at every man who passed.

There was a hammering from the middle of the square and I saw three bodies were laying in the clay and mud. Their scalps were missing. The Coffin Maker locked eyes with me when he knelt to take the corpses' measurements. We held each other's gaze for a long time, a small smile settled on his face as he nodded and I nodded back.

Jake had been a scout, sharpshooter as well it turned out, and he wasn't one to miss things. "Someone you know?"

I wondered what to tell him, how much to tell him. I couldn't have him talking to the Coffin Maker. Decided that the barest truth would be best. "Old acquaintance. I want you to take the coach to the outskirts. Keep a sharp eye; this isn't the place to leave things unguarded, even your life."

Jake nodded, his iron strapped tight to his hip. I'd let him handle the repeater a few times. I advised him that gun was going to be his friend in the next few hours he was alone.

"Miss Holloway, I want you to get up to the local poke hole, ask if they have any reckoning of where Sergeant Earnest Craft might be."

Ruby nodded and asked, "What will you be doing?"

I looked over at the Coffin Maker, still taking measurements of the last body. I made sure the Gun was on my hip; it comforted me when I looked at the man. "Going to be reconnecting." I urged Tobias on, hearing Jake do the same with Soldier and Maestro.

The coffin maker didn't turn as I sauntered up, cautiously dismounting and waiting while he finished his work. He took a deep breath, scratching at his chin, "Been a while. Time gets a little fuzzy for me, but I do know that."

It had been nearly fifteen years, sixteen even.

"Different line of work than when I last saw you," I said.

The coffin maker chuckled lightly, pulling a few slots of wood onto his work bench, hammer in hand as he positioned the nail. "It's still the same line of work, Salem, just a different area is all. I trade in death . . . just like you." He began to hammer and Tobias nickered and shook his head, backing away behind me. "You came for the Yankee Sergeant? Don't look so shocked; you know I've kept tabs on you since we parted. Quite a career, quite a lot of bodies. Made my old heart proud!"

I didn't have any doubt of that; a coffin maker needed bodies to be kept in business. I hadn't seen this particular one on my trail over the years, but I wouldn't have been surprised if he'd been following behind me, picking up the pieces and making sure the dead had places to rest.

One part of the coffin was ready, I smelled fresh pine, and the Coffin Maker walked around and placed another board into position. "You'll have a fight on your hands, even with your weapon. Sergeant Craft has made many friends in my circles," he said fixing me with a knowing look, his black pupils off put by the bags under his eyes that were rubbed raw, like his skin wasn't agreeing to the cool air.

He didn't have to impress on me the implications of that, or who else was backing Sergeant Craft. I knew them well enough, probably had met a few in my time. As it stood, they wouldn't stand between me and my vengeance.

"He does good work for us, damn good work. Real imaginative with pain, you know. Almost as good as you, but then again, you have been my best horse in the race."

He finished the sideboard, walking around to begin work on the footboard. I watched him for a moment, marveling at how the sallow skin, and stringy black hair, barely disguised what was beneath. Sometimes a sick soul couldn't be disguised. Then again, most people who did business up at the boot hill weren't altogether healthy.

"You know where I might find Sergeant Craft? My associates are looking for him, but you've been in town longer. Reckon that'll save us a whole mess of trouble."

I asked my question, but the Coffin Maker just chuckled darkly. "I ain't in the business of doing favors, Salem, you know that. You've known it ever since you and Virgil called on me. There was a price for that just like there would be a price for this." He paused his hammering for a moment to watch me as my finger tapped the Gun, trying to find a way to work the information out of him. "Is that a bluff, Salem? Or do you mean it for a real play?" He chuckled and pointed a finger at the brand below my eye. "That's why you're going to kill Earnest Craft, son. Killer instinct, selfish desire, bloodlust that drenches everything. I saw it even back then when you were nothing but a juniper popping out of the soil. That's why I gave you that mark there, my mark."

The brand itched, badly, like I'd rubbed damn poison ivy over it.

The Coffin Maker went back to his work. I stepped up and reluctantly took my hand away from the Gun. He glanced up at me with a curious expression, almost protective of the box that he carved. "You've got a lot of debt still, but maybe we can work something out. Help me finish this and we'll talk."

My hands found themselves grasping the wood as he hammered, talking absentmindedly about old times, and about people, some of whom I knew and some who were long dead.

When we finished making the footboard. He took a step back to admire his handwork. He flourished the brown leather coat, old seams stitched from where the elements had their way. This man was a perfect craftsman. Sure, it wasn't a coffin like some rail baron or swell from New York would expect, but for folks living on the edge it would have been better than most.

"Magnificent, isn't it? Not as swell as the one you're carrying around on the back of your coach, but close." The Coffin Maker wiped his hands and turned to look at me with a small smile. "Brings us to business, then. I'd like to take the fancy box off your hands, contents included." He smiled and gestured towards the surrounding town. "People would pay good money to see a dead redskin; the Sioux have been raiding us frequently. In return, I'll give you Earnest Craft, even throw in the Weber brothers and Lamb."

My interest was piqued, my entire vendetta offered up to me on a platter. It was almost too good to be true. But I'd been on the receiving end of this before, and even if there was danger keeping my teacher around, I wasn't going to turn him over to be some sideshow exhibit for rubes. "Sorry, appreciate the offer, but I'm in this until the end. You'll see them all adorned in pine, be it tomorrow or months from now. I aim to put all of them under."

The Coffin Maker chuckled and shrugged his shoulders. "If you want to hang on to the old troublemaker, that is your choice. He'll keep until you're ready to turn him into the ground."

I nodded. Couldn't tell if he was lying or not; the people of boot hill loved their stiffs.

The Coffin Maker yawned; it was massive, over drawn, like he thought this was supposed to be what a man who was tired would do. "The hour's getting late and I think I'm ready to get into the liquor. And you have hunting to do." He patted my shoulder as he passed me, sending gooseflesh prickling under my sleeve. "You've always been a card, Salem; more grit in you than a thousand men. That's why I know you'll finish paying off what you and your brother owe." His black eyes panned to the Gun in its holster, strangely silent. "Never would have made that for you if I didn't think you couldn't hold up your end."

He tipped his hat to me and, in the blink of an eye; I thought I saw the skin beneath it writhing with maggots. Then he brought it back up.

I tipped my hat in return and turned away, walking back to Tobias and letting my mind wander back to old techniques to control fear. The mind plays tricks and sometimes coffin makers were just that.

I couldn't spot him in the crowd of men heading toward the saloon. Of course, I hadn't really expected to.

CHAPTER ELEVEN

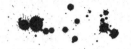

"CRAFT IS OUT on patrol with a cavalry unit. Sioux attacks have been rampant and a few of the locals have been killed," Ruby said, she had returned halfway through the night.

Jake had parked the coach on a hill overlooking the town. Fires burning in lanterns and tents sprinkled the gulch and distant sounds of laughter and debasement came from the saloon.

Ruby sat down next to him, rubbing her hands together. "Pass me a cup of Arbuckle's, Jake. I swear some of the men in this town act like they haven't had a poke in months."

Jake poured out the cup of coffee, the brew steaming in the night as he passed the mug into Ruby's grateful hands. She sipped slowly and I waited patiently for her to finish.

I had been laboring on a few new workings, mixing hoodoo and other disciplines I'd learned. It was for peace of mind; even if I couldn't be killed by a gun, there was nothing that said my companions couldn't fall to the same. It would be inconvenient for me if Jake caught a bullet and I had to take a jaunt to the other side every time I needed information.

"None of the girls knew much about his schedule. He's been kicked out of the saloon, you see. Cut up a girl so bad that she had to leave the line of work; none of the Johns could stand the sight of her. They had so many stories about him, but nothing about where he is now."

I finished tying the bit of string around the red bag and quietly asked my next request. "Tell me the stories."

Ruby looked confused, but I picked up another bit of cloth that I had taken from a saloon and began the same process, gesturing for her to continue. She told me about Sergeant Craft, at least the offhand descriptions of him she had obtained from the working girls. I pictured him in my mind: stocky, a beard that was untrimmed and scraggly that hung to his chest. He would have scars; his uniform was from ten years ago, though he wore it with pride.

I had shut my eyes, trying to picture the man, building everything from the small crook in his nose from a Dixie man's battlefield struggles to the healed scar on his shoulder where a rifle had found its mark. He would smell, Ruby made that clear. All the whores had dreaded to service him no matter how hard his money was. Sergeant Craft loved the smell of blood, an indulgence I could sympathize with. Apparently, the good military man never washed it off his clothes and would go days between bathing after he'd killed a man.

This was fine knowledge, a fine story, one that I would enjoy sweating out of the good sergeant once I had my hands on him. Ruby was still talking; the ladies in the saloon must have been quick to chirp with the amount of details she was able to give me, but I had enough to formulate a plan.

"Thank you, Miss Holloway. You've given me more than enough to work with. I can track him down with that."

She picked up the coffee again, sipping it quietly with a knowing smile. I'd played enough bad hands of poker to know when I was being set up. "Is there something else you would like to tell me?"

Ruby rolled her shoulders, the dress emphasizing her breasts as she leaned back and took a deep breath of the night air. "Took a few rolls with some clients while I was there. Made good money, enough that we can get some proper vittles while we're here, but wouldn't you know it? The coffin maker, the one you were talking to earlier, Mr. Covington? He was all willing to talk after he'd had a poke."

Panic seized me and the working that I'd been preparing fell apart at my hands as my fingers clenched my pants, near white as the blood ran from them. I could feel the mocking laughter on the back of my neck, same kind of laughter that hucksters used when some rube had fallen into the ages old set up.

"Did you—" I cleared my throat, trying to calm my heart that was pounding like a whole herd of cattle. "Did you promise anything else? Anything other than the poke?"

The woman looked confused, her green eyes searching mine and wondering what would happen if she answered in a way that didn't agree with me. "No, he just wanted the poke. I thought you'd sent him to me. He paid hard money for it." She produced a gold piece from the folds of her dress and offered it to me with a shaking hand.

"Look at that piece," I said, cutting her off mid-gab and pointing at the coin she held in her hand. Jake leaned in from his spot, eager to be involved and see just what had my nerves rattled. The coin bore the same mark as the one beneath my eye.

Both of my companions stared at my eye and Ruby dropped the gold piece into the dirt. She was panicking as I stood, crawling off the log and into the grass and mud, uncaring of her pretty dress being stained. "I didn't . . . I didn't know that . . . "

Jake stepped between us, hand twitching towards his piece. "She didn't know who the man was. I didn't know, either. You can't go killing her for ignorance, Mr. Covington."

I chuckled. It was amusing to see how close Ruby had come to being like me. One small tip of the scale and it would be her wandering the wastes of America looking for another soul to kill.

The coin had landed close to the fire. It burned at my fingertips as I picked it up, but I didn't mind it much. Fire had left much more permanent marks on me. "You assume I mean to harm either of you, but I made promises to you, Mr. Howe. Might be the reason you're getting uppity, but you shouldn't worry . . . " I shoved past him and offered my hand to Ruby. She took it reluctantly. "Neither of you have led a story worth ending yet."

When she was back on her feet, I handed her the coin. She had earned it; let her spend it how she would. Gold was the currency of the soul and drove the madness around these hills.

"You've done good work, Miss Holloway, and with that, I release you from my service. You're free to leave if you'd like, or stay and continue to travel with Mr. Howe and I. It doesn't matter to me, but before you make that decision . . . tell me what the Coffin Maker said to you."

Ruby put the coin away and looked directly into my eye, and then at the Gun strapped to my hip. "You're not just saying that? I'm not going to be walking down this hill and hear a shot that lays me down with the angels?"

I chuckled and nodded. "It's a promise; you'll leave this town alive."

"Guess I have no choice then, huh?" she laughed. I grew impatient, but I let her have her moment as she stared at the coin in her hand, no doubt wondering what she had traded away or what that symbol really meant. "He said that Craft has a secret place, outside Deadwood. It's not much more than a foundation now, an old settler house that the Sioux burned down, but it still has a basement."

Ruby stopped for a moment, the gold coin flipping between her fingers as she composed herself. "He takes people there, does things to them. The Coffin Maker said that most people that live close to this place hear the screams." She shuddered, but an understanding passed between us, the iron that she carried in her soul mingling with the sulfur that flowed through mine.

"He's a bad man, Mr. Covington, slime of the earth. I know you mean to put him down just like you did Maddox. It's going to make things better and avenge a lot of folks."

I gave her a devil's grin. "Of that you can be certain, Miss Holloway."

She licked her lips. She'd heard parts of my conversation with Dead Bear, what I had done to John Maddox and Mr. Bradford. I wondered if she now had pity for the men in my path, maybe fear for herself, fear that she would wind up inside another bison corpse suffocating as the sun rose and baked the dead ruin until she burned.

"He didn't say when he would be back there, but that he didn't stay away long, a few days at most. The girls . . . they told me what he did . . . to the whore he cut up, what she looks like now."

Ruby told me these things, information that I would put to use, and then I tipped my hat to her. "Go in peace if you want. Take Tobias, the horse needs a good home. Or stay, ride with us as long as you're able or wanting. As for me, I have the business of death to be about, and Mr. Howe will be accompanying me."

With those last words to her, I retreated until I was behind the stagecoach, at Dead Bear's coffin. I unfastened the chains that kept it in place and listened as Jake made his overtures to Ruby.

"Do you really mean to leave?" Jake was trying to whisper, but with only the crackling of the small fire, there wasn't much use in hiding his conversation.

"Jake, I'm grateful for what you've done for me; you saved me from the noose and I'm not ever going to forget that . . . "

I glanced around the coach to see she was stroking his face before she saddled the deceased marshal's horse. Ironic that she would ride the steed of the man that had condemned her.

"You ever run into me and want a free roll, I'll be happy to give it up to you, but him . . . " No illusions there who she was speaking about. "He's going to kill you, Jake. I think he'll kill everyone he meets someday. I- I can't be one of them. I'm afraid of him, afraid of his kindness just as much as his anger. I'm going back east; don't think Salem is going to follow anyone there."

Harsh words, not necessarily untrue.

"Take care, Jake, and remember what I said." With that warning, she urged Tobias on and was gone; a clatter of hoof beats echoing on the hills and disappearing just as quick.

I gave him a moment before I called out. "Mr. Howe, if you don't mind assisting, we have work to do."

CHAPTER TWELVE

WE SPENT THE next two days searching for Sergeant Craft's secret abode. I had heard of men like this, those who found hidden places to work pain on people. They never stopped, one death was never enough. The hunger would well up again and they'd go out into the night looking for something to sate it. I sympathized with them; in my world or theirs, dealing death was just the way of things.

The burned down husk overlooked a hillside that had been picked clean, old stumps barely clinging to the grey clay that was all that remained from the barren hillside. The burnt shells of logs were all that remained of the house that had once stood here, black and charred ash giving away Craft's comings and goings. I knelt in that ash, measuring the size of the boot prints and feeling the ancient stone where blood had dried.

Jake brought two lanterns from the coach, handing one to me. The hair on the back of my neck stood on end, goose flesh prickling its way down my arms. I drew the Gun, Jake's own piece already in his hand. I put one finger to my lips and gestured to the trail. It ended in a locked cellar and from somewhere between the wooden slats, I saw a light burning.

"You think he's down there?"

No point in telling him to be silent, not with the lock on the cellar. There was only one way to get through those doors. I aimed carefully and slowly pulled the trigger.

There was a clap of thunder, pained metal, and the lock went tumbling into the grass. I motioned for Jake to pull the doors apart. If Craft was down there waiting, I'd rather him take a shot at me than be dead on and put my companion under.

Jake heaved, gritting his teeth as he pulled the heavy wood back. I braced myself, expecting to hear gunfire and make a few corpses, but nothing moved down in the dark except the small flickering of a solitary candle.

"He might not have come back yet, but someone sure has." Jake spoke truth, one that brought me to a crossroads. This hole needed exploring, no doubt about that, but more than likely there was going to be gunplay, and an awfully big risk that Jake would catch a bullet.

Still, I couldn't kill Mr. Craft, not without trying to divine some information from him, and his face was still unknown to me. No choice at all, really.

"Mr. Howe, stay behind me. If someone starts shooting, you let me kill them."

Jake nodded, moving in behind me as I descended into the cellar. Even with my instructions, he kept his weapon out. The floor was wet, rainfall seeping through the cellar doors and turning it into quagmire. It sucked at our boots, each step laborious and heavy. The candle burned on a small table. Someone had left a bandolier there, a few knives, and a pouch. It didn't look like they were expecting to be followed. Crouching in the muck, I noticed footprints leading further into the dark. Whoever had come before us was barefoot.

The cellar branched off in two directions, a dim passage to the right and another continuing straight.

"Want to split up?" Jake whispered.

I shook my head, gesturing for silence, and then closed my eyes, listening . . .

There was dripping water, rustling, and below that, a quiet and rhythmic grunting.

I pointed down the hallway to the right. Jake nodded, following my path as I proceeded as reserved as possible. We couldn't have gone far when I saw a new light flickering. I doused my lantern, Jake following my lead.

The passageway was a dead end, but on the left was a room. The light danced forth from the doorway and played merry hell with the shadows on the wall. There was a rhythmic and pleased grunting coming from inside the room.

I hoped that my slow pace would disguise the noise of the mud sucking at my boots. The wall was wet with moss and lichens; I felt them on my skin as I pushed myself against the wall and peered inside.

Boards had been placed over the mud, a few candles burned from a dresser and a nightstand, and there was a bed in the center of the room. A dead woman lay on it, her eyes staring blankly at the ceiling while the man dressed in a soiled cavalry uniform shoved his pecker into her stomach.

She was a Negro, her olive skin nearly as dark as

the night, she'd been cut on. I could see the wounds and her insides, bits of bone and pink meat.

The man on top of her bucked and writhed as he thrusted into her, the skin pulled tight as his pecker burrowed inside like a fat worm. Her head flopped and those dead eyes stared at me. There was no story there, no connection; her soul had already made flight to whatever waited on the other side. Maybe it would be pearly gates; seemed the only decent thing considering her slaughter.

I couldn't say the same for her killer.

The filth kept pumping away as I stepped into the room, never letting up as he turned his face to the sky, his eyes squeezed shut in ecstasy.

My hand grasped around his throat and I heaved backward, sending him flying ass-over-end into the floor. I pressed the Gun into his head, his eyes twirling up to look at the barrel pressed between them. His pecker was hanging out of his trousers and his chest was bare, only the blue coat of a 2nd Cavalryman hanging off his shoulders. He threw his hands up, putting them out to shield himself, like they would somehow protect him from the bullet I so desperately wanted to put in him.

"Oh Christ . . . " Jake muttered, his eyes looking at the dead woman on the bed before flicking to the man whimpering on the floor. I saw his eyes become hard and he walked over to the man, shoving past me and striking him across the face with one solid blow. "You son of a bitch! You rancid shit stain son of a bitch!"

The man's scalp was bleeding, red lines running down his skin to mix with the wild and unkempt beard. Jake shot his revolver into the floor, chunks of wood flying as the man covered his face. I detected the strong scent of piss and the man released onto the floor, his legs balling up under him as he made noises like a newborn goat.

Jake pressed the hot barrel into the man's cheek and he screamed. Jake's hand immediately struck, wrapping around the man's face to keep him from pulling him away.

I watched all of this with a sense of pride. I'd seen plenty of men try to emulate others, or let that righteous anger take them over the edge where the darkness would whisper to them and I wondered which one Jake was indulging in.

The barrel cooled and the man fell back, grasping at the ugly black wound oozing red with blood, the smell of cooked skin filling the small room. Jake stood panting and I reached out to grasp his shoulder. He seemed to jump in place then looked at me with wide eyes.

I knew this look, the one where a man realized he'd slipped, gone further, wasn't the hero of their little story. No one was a hero; such a thing didn't exist, and in time, Jake would realize that too.

"I applaud the assistance, Mr. Howe. Am I to assume that this isn't Sergeant Craft?" It was almost moronic to ask; a man of Craft's reputation wouldn't have been sitting around crying his eyes out and begging not to die. At least, not with the small amount of pain he'd received so far.

Jake shook his head. "Nah, I don't have a clue who this shit stain is."

I didn't smile, though I sorely wanted to. You could

practically smell the foul deeds that the man shivering in the pool of his own piss had entertained. My soul was a twisted trail, sulfur and pain-wielding death everywhere I went, and I'd killed more than my fair share of innocents. But it never felt old, paying evil unto evil.

My boot splashed in the puddle of piss as I squatted to look the man in the eye. I saw the recognition in his eye when he caught sight of the brand. I managed to rustle a few words from between his panicked lips.

"You . . . you're Covington."

Couldn't place his accent, might have been from back east; sick bastard who couldn't cut it in the city and went looking for his appetites elsewhere. "Hit the nail on the head. Now if you would be so kind, what is your name?"

The man shook his head, the mop of black hair on his head throwing bits of sweat everywhere. "Please, I don't want to die. I've don—"

The Gun whispered to me and my anger sizzled like grease in the skillet. I pointed my weapon at his pecker. "I know what you've done, but make no mistake, we're going to kill you. I can't let a man who pokes dead women stay above ground."

The man whimpered, begging for mercy, but he wouldn't be finding any with me, not this night.

"The manner of your passing, how painful that is, that's up to you. Might even let you ask for forgiveness from the Good Lord, if I'm so inclined . . . But if you refuse me your name one more time, I'm going to shoot off your dick and force feed it to you."

The man blubbered and wiped his face and then told me that his name was Roscoe Olson.

"Thank you, Mr. Olson. Now if you would be so kind as to tell us why you're down here fucking a dead woman?"

He talked; defeated men often did. Very few men had the backbone to keep their secrets to themselves when they were promised pain beyond their wildest imaginings.

Sergeant Craft had spread his bloody desires to other members of his unit. Technically he'd mustered out of the army, but he'd been sought after by the military units here, helping them keep the Sioux at bay. He'd preached his gospel that the white man was king and everything else was less: black women, Chinamen, native children . . . all of them existed to serve or die. In Craft's mind, the two could be combined into his favorite pastime: inflicting pain.

Funny. That was my favorite game, too.

"They told me I only had to keep watch! Use the merchandise how I wanted. I-no one was supposed to find us!" His wailing and blubbering were beginning to scratch the part of me that wondered at the use of keeping him alive, but I had more questions.

"Thank you, Mr. Olson. Now, how many people have bought into Sergeant Craft's appetites and when will they be back?"

I asked it simply, but he shook his head. "I don't want to die!"

This time I laughed, long and hard. Then I stepped onto his penis and pressed it into the wood. He screamed and desperately pulled at my boot, trying to dislodge my foot from his organ. "Sergeant Craft isn't here. I'm sure you're speaking truth about the terrible things he'd do to you, but he doesn't have my imagination."

I reached down and wound my hand through his hair, gesturing for Jake to attend to the dead woman on the bed. "Take her to the cellar doors. We'll bury her when our business here is done. Mr. Olson has decided that he would rather take the way of pain than the way of truth. No chance for pleading with this one, and I'd rather you still be able to sleep after the night is through, Mr. Howe."

Jake silently and reverently picked up the woman's body, then looked at me as I dragged Olson toward the bed. "I don't think I'm going to sleep well for a few drives, Salem." He left, gingerly carrying the woman.

I threw Olson onto the bed, drawing my knife and stabbing into his hand. Blood bubbled from the wound and his screams were like gravy over morning biscuits.

Olson gibbered, staring at the ceiling and shaking his head. "Our Father, who art in heaven—"

My fist met his nose and I felt the bone crunch under my fingers. "He's still in heaven, Mr. Olson, but I'm here."

He'd bitten into his tongue. Blood churned up from his ruined mouth and he tried wrenching his hand from the knife but only bawled louder.

"Time to die, Mr. Olson."

CHAPTER THIRTEEN

JAKE COVERED HIS ears when I had begun to
work on Olson. He would describe it to me
later, saying that it sounded like some lost soul, crying
for heaven. He heard wet noises, an occasional laugh,
and then one long howl before silence.

Olson had talked, and Sergeant Craft would be
returning in the morning. He'd also elaborated on
another room in this cellar, and no amount of pain
that I could inflict on this man quenched the sickness
rolling around in my stomach from that knowledge.
When there was nothing left of Olson but a pile of
flesh and ruined meat, I took my leave and walked
back down the passageway.

Olson had been a local man, one of the first people
from Deadwood to buy into Craft's fantasies and
delusions when he had come to town.

I slid the man's tongue into my pocket. There hadn't
been much to take, but I was sure that I could use his
mutilated organ in some way or another. Even if I had
made sure he died hard, what Roscoe had said was
waiting at the end of this hall didn't fill me with joy.

To the left was Jake and the cellar doors, but to
the right . . .

I took a deep breath and made my way deeper. It opened up into a larger dugout, but there were no wooden boards here, just the sucking mud and the clinking of chains. A few cages were stuck fast into the dirt, flies congregating on the corpses within. Some bodies hung loosely from the ceiling, shackles over their wrists, men and women, all in various states of death, all of them bearing the marks of Craft's work.

There was a dead woman, her face still frozen in her last scream. I put a hand to her flesh only to feel cold. Blood stained her naked body from where her breasts had been cut off. A man lay face down on the table. He too had not been afforded dignity; his unclothed back had been ripped apart and his ribs and organs pulled out through the yawning hole.

I heard a groan from the corner of the room. I whirled and pointed my Gun directly at the monster standing tall at the other end of the room. It lunged forward, groaning and bleeding from multiple cuts spread across its body. Swollen breasts dangled towards the wrinkled belly, but its head . . .

The thing had the head of a pig, massive tongue lolling out of its mouth as its hands reached for me.

The Gun practically shouted in my head and my finger closed over the trigger as I backed up into a corpse of a man hanging from the chains. Only thing that kept me from sending this thing back on down to hell was the fact that it fell to its knees groveling when it saw the Gun.

I'd let my senses get muddied, let them take leave and fly. I wasn't the victim; I was the wolf waiting in the dark. I'd failed to reckon the stitches holding the pig's head in place and the fact what I had mistaken for squeals were the gibberish pleadings of whoever was behind that pig's head.

Veins stood out against the woman's skin, a mass of wrinkles, and I could see a small smattering of thin grey hair sticking out from beneath the pig's head. A thick iron collar hung on her neck, the chain leading back to the wall.

I holstered the Gun, letting the piece scream into my mind. I gritted my teeth; the weapon was growing hungrier for death each day, and Olson hadn't quenched its thirst.

"Calm down, I'm going to get that thing off of you." I said as I got closer.

The woman whimpered, the pig's head making it sound like a snort. I pulled my knife and walked towards her slowly, hands raised. The threadwork had been crude, ugly purple and yellow spreading out from the stitches, and the pig flesh had begun to rot.

"I'm going to cut through the thread. Try not to move or you'll be breathing through a new neck hole."

The woman said something; might've been agreeing, might've been begging me not to do it, but I began the labor of removing the decapitated animal's head all the same. Thread came apart easily enough, but the occasional twitch sent my blade nicking into her abused and spoiled flesh. The woman whined and bits of blood and white pus ran down her skin.

I cut through the last stitch, putting away my knife and reaching out to remove the putrefying sow head. Bits of blood and flesh came away and the face of an old woman appeared, covered with spittle and maggots.

The dead swine's dome landed in the mud and

rolled, hollow dark spots where eyes once had been staring out at us.

"Thank you, mister!" The woman said, tears trickling down dirty cheeks. "Thank you!"

My soul was devoid of conscience, and I'd long ago imprisoned any decency I possessed, but from its cell somewhere deep and dark, I could still hear it whisper louder than the Gun sometimes.

I wrapped my coat around the old woman and brought her to her feet. "Miss, my name is Salem Covington and I have business with the man who did this to you."

When I was little, my mother would read to my brother and I. She'd read us one about an old hag in the woods, this woman in front of me was how I always imagined she'd look. And where I could see where beauty had once lived in her features, that'd been worn away with her time under the rotting head of a pig.

"You mean to kill him?" She asked, coughing spittle into her hand.

"Yes ma'am, after he answers a few questions."

The old woman had risen onto shaking feet, gesturing to the collar. "Get me out of this thing, I'll help you strangle the bastard; it's my fault for all the pain he's eked out on folks."

I gave her a curious look. She saw the brand under it, nodding as if that explained everything, then she gave me the first interesting fact I'd collected in a long time.

"I'm his mother."

The sun was coming up swollen like a red tick. I waited just below the entrance to the cellar. Dead Bear's coffin sat next to me. I'd told him my plan, hoping that he could hear me from wherever he was, and explained his role in it. The deep growl and resounding thumps from the inside of the coffin told me he approved.

Jake and I had found clothing for Mrs. Craft. I'd taken my coat back and relished the scent of fouled wounds and unwashed body. Now, the two of them waited on the hill overlooking the burned-down home.

I sat on the cellar steps, listening as the distant sound of hoof beats drew closer and smiled when I heard someone shout, "The hell is this!?"

They'd discovered their victims, piled in a nice heap in front of the cellar door. It was the best way to keep Craft and his posse in one place. I heard movement, boot prints in the dirt, obviously coming to check what had been left for them.

Jake had been furious when I told him my plan, but I had won out in the end. Mrs. Craft had been quite persuasive in convincing him that this was a good way to go about killing.

I hoped that Earnest Craft was made of tough stuff.

Pressing down on the plunger, I created miniature thunder. And pain.

The dynamite I had planted under the pile of flesh worked well; splattered limbs, earth, and rock were sent flying over the remote gulch. As the blast echo died away, it was replaced by the screams of agonized men.

WILE E. YOUNG

The smell of charred flesh and fresh blood hit my nose as I rose from the darkness of the cellar. Two men lay on the ground, one missing a leg, the other clutching his belly to keep his guts inside. A dozen other men picked themselves up off the ground, their horses having run to find greener pastures.

Standing like they had just been kicked in the head by a horse, were three men and two women. Rope bound their hands; most of them looked lost, panicked, a few already had bruises and blood leaked out of the bottom of the youngest girl's dress.

Devil save me, but these were men it was a pleasure to kill. I breathed deep, and the Gun sang.

The man holding his guts twitched twice, his eyes looking down briefly at the new holes I'd put in his stomach. The one without a leg looked up with pained eyes. His mind had scattered and he obviously wasn't thinking straight when he asked, "Please mister, I'm hurt."

I shot him through the head; didn't bother wasting time.

The men had gotten their act together, beginning to draw iron. One stumbled a few feet and fired. The bullet went far too wild.

"Gentleman! Normally, I'd ask you for your names, your stories . . . "

Two more straightened, fired. One bullet hit the dirt in front of me while the other tore a new hole through my coat.

"But Roscoe has told me all of that, each one of your sins laid bare. He sang like a songbird."

More of them fired, more misses. I could not be killed by a gun.

"Hell has made sure you've eaten well, but the feast is over and the tab has come due," I roared, ancient words pouring from me as I extended the Gun and fired twice.

Two men caught the shots. The first man's left eye popped like a bubble on the surface of water, blood running down his face as he pawed at his now missing sight.

The second shot drove through the next man like a knife through butter. I saw the misty spray of red as it came out of his back. He looked afraid when he coughed thick globs of near black blood, reaching out with one hand and then dropping to his side in a heap.

Maybe I'd seen my way through too many slaughters, or maybe it was like the Coffin Maker had said and other powers were at work to preserve these dispensers of torment.

The smoke from the dynamite drifted high into the trees, carrying the smell of cooked flesh over the wind. When I stepped next to it, I heard footsteps.

Boots pounded in the dirt and Sergeant Earnest Craft emerged from the smoke, hands outstretched to either side. I didn't have time to turn before he grabbed me up in a death grip and took me to the ground. We hit the dirt hard, his hand wrapping around the bones in my wrist, tight, too tight, I felt my grip loosen . . .

The Gun stopped whispering, bouncing away through the dirt.

Overconfidence; I'd been steeped in it for years. Killed enough folks that I was damn sure that I'd lost the ability to be afraid. I could practically hear the Coffin Maker laughing as Earnest Craft grinned down at me, drool dripping through the gaps between his teeth.

"Stand down, boys! Got me a big worm here." The man was strong. I managed to wrangle a hand out, but my fist did little more than draw a scrape on his cheek. "Expected more from a man like you, Covington."

Metal kissed leather and the knife was in his hand, pressing against my throat. It took a supreme effort not to flick my eyes up to the hill where Jake and Sergeant Craft's mother waited. I may have thought of myself as a real curly wolf, but this time I'd been properly bushwhacked. Surety would kill a fellow just as easily as a bullet.

I stared up at Sergeant Craft, stringy grey hair hung off his mostly bald head, dirt and grit sticking to a sweat stained face.

"Don't worry, Covington. I'm not going to kill you, not yet."

I stared back impassively, setting my lip straight, trying to act like his words didn't affect me.

His men appeared next to him and they dragged me to my feet. Most of them didn't look much different than their commander with ragged uniforms and lecherous grins.

"Pretty gun." One of the men stepped up and reached down, plucking the Gun from the ground. "Think it might be worth something, boss?"

"Older model, but that's Salem Covington's gun. Hand it here."

I lost my temper when I saw the man hand my weapon over to Craft. I lunged forward and attempted to take a chunk out of his throat. My teeth closed around a bit of his beard hair, oily to the taste, and he hollered when his men wrenched me back, taking a small patch out of his chin and leaving small trickles of blood behind.

His fist rearranged my jaw and sent small trickles of black, like little flies, floating in my vision. Where was Jake?

"Salem! SALEM!"

I knew that voice, but I'd never heard it filled with that much concern before. I turned my head; Jake had his hands over his head. Miss Craft had the rifle pointed directly into his back.

Another stupid mistake; I'd been blinded by the sense that I was playing the hero for once, and missed the fundamental truth of it all . . .

Mothers love their children.

"Little birdies were itching to put you under, but old flannel mouth there thought he could euchre you up good," Mrs. Craft said.

Earnest Craft smiled, glancing at me as I shrugged, spitting blood. "What can I say? I didn't take you for a man who was graced with an overabundance of thinking." I gave him my most devil-may-care grin. Angry people make mistakes and I wasn't ready to fold my hand.

Mrs. Craft sidled up next to her son. Craft leaned down and kissed her full on the mouth like she was a prize filly and he was trying to put the mash on her. When he finally came up for air, he gestured with his knife toward the cellar. "Take 'em both and get 'em strung up." He looked at Jake. "Do what you want with him, but leave Covington for me."

He patted his mother on her backside and she

grinned up at him. He smiled back before locking eyes with me. "I've got business first, but I'll save some playtime for you, Covington."

CHAPTER FOURTEEN

JAKE'S SCREAMS OF agony mixed well with Craft's moans of pleasure. It drifted down the tunnel, finding us surrounded and in chains. They'd stripped us down to our union suits, tearing Jake's to pieces with a knife.

That same knife was currently slicing through his nipple. He howled and jumped, dark blood running down his chest.

A hot knife came next, blade heated over an open flame. The smell made my stomach rumble. Jake made a noise at the back of his throat, halfway between a cat purring and a gurgle as he choked on his saliva. His eyes rolled back in his head and he slumped unconscious.

"Hot damn, he lasted longer than the last bitch we had in here, remember her? The whore from Iowa? Best pair of tits I've ever worked on!" The soldier laughed as I glared. They'd strung up their other prisoners: two men, a girl who couldn't have been more than eight, an old man, and one woman. Four of the soldiers had immediately gone to drinking, while the other two had gone to work on their prizes

They'd already killed one of the men; the sounds

of his caterwauling had reached a crescendo like a screaming cougar when they'd taken a pair of scissors to his balls, blood sloughing out onto the ground slowly. His teeth had been taken one by one. Cut off his eyelids too before he'd finally let himself fall back into that comforting void. I'd seen his chest stop moving after they began to work on his fingers. Bled to death while unconscious. Could've been worse; he could've been awake for it.

This was their way apparently; kill one hard and fast, get the blood pumping, while they thought up new and interesting ways to make sure the rest died screaming. A process I could mighty respect if I wasn't on the other end of it.

The men passed around the bottles and I waited. Shouldn't be long now, I'd left it easy enough for them to find.

Craft wandered in with his mother, bare feet splattering through the mud. He was covered with what I'd left of Roscoe Olson. I could smell the shit and piss on him as he came toward me. His mother's hair was askew, holding onto the wall for comfort. She was wearing my coat now, and nothing else.

"Have to thank you, Covington. Not often I've had a poke on top of a dead man, or at least what's left of him."

I didn't respond. I looked past him to the dark tunnel. Thought I could hear scraping.

Craft's smile wavered a little, but his mother folded into his arm as he reached out. "Mama always taught me that nothing was beyond us, every want and desire. Pain was just more pleasure, if you had the perspective of seeing it as such."

I heard footsteps, heavy, like they were struggling. "Mama likes the pain, don't you?"

His mother giggled like a schoolgirl in his arms, reaching up to flick a bit of drool out of his beard hair. "You sound just like your daddy when you say that!"

I worked my hand against the chain, whispering under my breath. Chain breaking was some of the oldest magic in the world.

"Salem?" Jake came back to the land of the living, his head rolling around on his neck as his eyes tried to focus on me.

"Mr. Howe, try not to scream. We will soon be far from here. I'll pay you more to compensate for your injury." It was a promise I intended to keep, but Craft definitely thought I was shooting my mouth off, trying to sound bigger. His laughter and that of his men silenced the whimpering sobs of their victims.

Keep laughing. Bigwigs down south might have wanted you to stay in the game, but they hadn't bothered to go about stacking the deck.

"You're a real act, Covington, big and scary. Your pal the shaman spoke about you." Craft danced merrily in the mud, waving one hand over his mouth and putting the other behind his head in the shape of feathers, whooping and hollering. "The Black Magpie, the Black Magpie, he'll come and kill you in the night." He devolved into laughter, his men following suit.

Only when it was finished, did I speak. "Funny you should mention my teacher, Mr. Craft, considering that I think your men might be bringing him in."

Earnest looked puzzled, then one of his men came, pulling and grunting, splattering the sides of Dead

Bear's coffin with mud. "Hey, Sarge, found this at the entrance. Think it belongs to him," the man said, pointing at me.

Craft clapped his hands together. He looked like a balding kid who'd just been told that his favorite toys were coming on the next coach.

"Well it's a small world! It's really him, Covington? You went and got him off that godforsaken piece of dirt we left him on?"

I didn't bother answering him, keeping my face stoic.

"Keep your trap shut all you want; easy enough to find out for myself. Boys, open it up. I want to piss on a dead redskin."

Sometimes, you plan things from the start, but other times it's all up to providence to see whether you catch a bullet or live to suck breath for another day.

And sometimes, an idiot is just an idiot.

One of Craft's men cut through the chains. I'd have to replace those when we were through. Then they pulled the coffin lid back.

I saw Jake flinch beside me, glancing over at me trying to control his pained gasps. Couldn't help the grin that was splitting my face from ear to ear.

Craft took no notice as he leered at Dead Bear's body. "Shit, Covington. Whatever heathen rites you used on him, it did the job good. It's been months since I skinned his head and looks like he died yesterday."

Dead Bear's eyes stared up furiously, the firelight from the torches reflecting off the lifeless pupils. He'd kept good in the time I'd traveled with him, his body unmarred by rot or fly.

I saw Mrs. Craft shiver as she stared down at my teacher, plucking at her son's arm. "Just hurry up, Earnest. I don't like the way he's looking up at me."

Craft reached over and hugged his mother close. He glanced over his shoulder at me. "Have to thank you, Covington. Not often I get to put an uppity Injun in his place twice."

There was a crash from somewhere down the hall and a breeze came through the tunnel. The prisoners immediately began to holler for help before a few rough blows silenced them.

Craft growled as he pulled away, slamming the coffin lid shut and stuffing his pecker back into his pants. "Hines, sounds like the wind got the doors flapping again. Go fix it."

A man with a short-cropped beard turned from where he'd been caressing the tied woman's breasts. He looked down the length of the hallway, at the shadows that seemed to be lengthening and stretching out. His chaps and cavalryman uniform hung loose from his form, like he was two sizes too small for it. He held his head as he stumbled forward, drunk as a skunk that'd found his way into the liquor cabinet. "You got it, Sarge. Take a look, get 'em quick like, be back for fun!" He was already soaked through with whatever whiskey they'd pilfered. He drew his piece and stumbled down the passageway, the dark swallowing him whole.

I turned my head to look at Jake. "When I make my move, you stand still and let me take care of it."

Jake looked at me like I'd gone soft in the head. "Salem, you're a monster with the Gun, but not even you can—"

There was a massive roar and a bloodcurdling scream and then nothing but the sound of wet tearing.

The mood immediately soured. Craft let go of his mother and the soldiers on a bender looked up in curiosity and alarm at the darkness of the tunnel. Craft stepped up closest, pistol drawn and ready as he swept it back and forth across the tunnel entrance.

"HINES!" he hollered, his voice echoing off the tunnels before falling silent. Then something heavy stepped into the wet mud. There were shuffling and grunting footsteps and heavy panting.

"Should have moved your death house once in a while, Craft!" I hollered. The man looked back at me, angry storms of thought and confusion running over his eyes. I gave him a grin that could have frightened the devil. "All this blood was sure to attract bears."

The massive grizzly appeared out of the tunnel, mouth opened in a yawning roar. Craft fell over the coffin trying to get away as I muttered the last words of my working. My hands came free of the shackles, I dove directly at the nearest man.

Gunshots flew from all directions and there was nothing around us but hollering. They never even noticed that I had slipped my restraints.

A man tried to drunkenly stumble past the bear, firing into its side with his piece. Might as well have been spitting for all it did him. A paw that could have removed a horse's head swiped down, claws separating skin from meat as they traveled across his flesh. The bear's paw was stained with red, the man held bits of his guts in his hands like they were chunks of wet bread.

The man fell against the muddy wall, hands

desperately clutching at the deep furrows, dark red blood pumping out with each beat of his terrified heart.

One of the soldiers crouched, firing toward the bear's head as it turned and placed one gigantic paw on the coffin lid, roaring in defiance, bits of red beginning to paint its fur.

I tackled the man, bashing his hand against the metal of the cage. I heard bones crack and his weapon dropped to the floor as the man desperately called for his companions to save him. None of them noticed, consumed with trying to put down the massive animal that had invaded their home.

No Gun to protect me. It was somewhere above in the soil; I could practically hear it calling. Even if I wanted to collect, needs must when the devil drives.

I closed my teeth around the man's throat; drawing blood and feeling the hard give of his trachea. His screams faded to gasps as he tried to push me off, but I was possessed of strength driven by vengeance. The skin stretched, and I thought I could almost hear the ripping like medicated paper as his throat came away in my mouth. I spit the flesh and blood out before I picked up his piece.

"BRING IT DOWN, KILL IT!" Craft's shouts of panic as he packed up through mud were practically lost, but I could hear it just fine.

The bear's mouth closed over a soldier's head. The man screamed and beat around the animal's muzzle until I heard a great crack as the man's hollering rose to a ringing wail. When the beast released him, his head was misshapen, the skull had caved in.

The dead man's gun had three shots still in the

cylinder. I pulled the hammer back and sent three men to an early death. Craft turned around at the gunshots, only for the butt of my gun to hit him square in the forehead. He went down like a toppling giant, thudding ass end into the mud.

"SARGE!" Craft's last man shouted. Wasn't sure if his piece was loaded or not, didn't rightly matter I suppose. The bear crawled over the coffin and took the man down in a deadly embrace.

I reached out with a trembling hand and leaned against the dirt wall, catching my breath. Mrs. Craft was sobbing as she tried to rouse her son, begging him to get up and defend her. He'd be getting back up, but she wasn't going to be around to see it.

The last man screamed, begged me to help, whimpered and called for his mother, then the bones in his neck snapped and the bear began to feast on his flesh. It was then that the begging began; the people that Craft and his posse had brought in, intended to work their depravity on, they all begged me for help, to not leave them there.

But nothing was louder than the voice in my mind; the Gun, calling me even through the dirt and concrete overhead, telling me how weak I was without it, how vulnerable . . .

I shook the thought and stood. The bear's head jutted up, muzzle covered in gristle and blood, a low growl escaping its mouth.

"Take your meal, wasape. Leave these. I'll bring the rest of the dead up when I finish my business."

One of the captives, the man, began to scream at me. "What the blasted hell are you doing? It's a fucking bear! Pick up a gun and—"

The bear turned and roared directly at him, rumbling forward on paws that could turn chain links into grits. The man whimpered and shrunk away from the animal, his closest compatriots doing likewise.

"Hey, HEY!" I yelled. The bear turned and looked at me. I locked eyes with it, wondering if there was a spark of intelligence there, if my teacher had crossed back over to help me avenge him.

Could have been him, but sometimes a bear was just a bear looking for a meal.

"Leave him. He doesn't know the ways like you and I. Take your meal and go." Even if I'd had the Gun, I was taking a gamble. The bear could have found his way inside, attracted to all the death that Craft had been so kindly dealing all these years. I whispered old words and incantations, protections, animal of spirit of my teacher temporarily flesh . . . there was a chance I wouldn't make it out alive.

The bear chuffed, blood dripping from its lower lip. I backed up as it turned away, taking the body of its freshest kill by the corpse's leg and dragging it off into the dark. I didn't breathe a sigh of relief until I heard those loud and thundering footfalls fade.

Craft had the keys. I took them from his pants and unlocked Jake's restraints. My companion curled his hands around his chest, breathing deep and trying not to show how much pain he was really in. Commendable. I tossed him the keys and he groaned as he reached to catch them, a small bit of ooze trickling from the charred flesh.

"Free the others, then we will dress your wound."

Jake looked at me like my bacon had slid off my plate, waving a hand at the rest of the people in chains. "Don't want to play God this time, Salem? No one to trade? I'm hurt, we're hurt, and instead of helping, you're going to what? Get your Gun, kill someone to make you feel better?"

I let him rant, the man deserved it. He'd been burdened with a lot on our journey, and now he'd been maimed. What he had seen in this place would have darkened lesser men. He didn't allow me to talk or offer any kind of explanation or assurance, and I could respect that, namely because there wasn't one. I'd been euchred and only managed to see the other side through the skin of my teeth.

"Clothe them. Keep them from killing Mrs. Craft." I said simply, turning to go.

Jake's glare matched my own this time. He had his chance to bring up his grievance, but now it was time to go about the devil's work. Jake could complain later. He backed down, shuffling over to the woman who was now crying tears of joy. I turned to Mrs. Craft and grinned, squatting in the mud until she could see the brand below my eye and the blood still staining my teeth.

"I believe you have my coat, ma'am."

CHAPTER FIFTEEN

THE GUN FELT good in my hand. I must have looked like a man desperate as I dug through the mud, following the whispering until I had found it. Returned my heartbeat to normal.

Now it beat with excitement as I looked at Craft, restrained in his own chains. His victims stood around me, clothed again in what little I had been able to provide, some even taking the uniforms of Craft's men.

The sergeant grinned. Even naked, at the mercy of people who undoubtedly wouldn't be granting him any, he still showed a bloody courage. "Nice job, Covington. Good way to turn it around with your dead heathen. Can't say that I know how you went about picking those locks, but a damn fine job."

This man had a way of prickling under my skin, like a damn splinter I just couldn't budge. I was used to men showing fear, giving into pain, but this man had made it clear . . . torture wasn't going to work on him.

Craft sank in his chains, cackling hard enough that it matched his mother next to him. Deprived of her coat, she was just as naked as her son; it wasn't a sight that was pleasing to the eye. Her body was covered in scars; old burn wounds, strokes from a whip, and what looked like teeth marks in places.

"Go ahead. Get to the pain! Send us off down the river!" He danced in his chains, his mother mimicking the motion and making obscene gestures at us as she gyrated her hips.

I stared at the both of them, trying to summon up any kind of cold that I still had in me after the sun had risen on this morning. "Going to ask you once, Craft. Where is August Lamb and the Weber brothers?"

Craft sighed, rolling his eyes and working his tongue in his gums. "Could we get to the killing already? I'm dying to see what they can cook up for me down south, see if hellfire is as hot as they say!"

"You heard him, Covington! Let's gut him!" It was the old man, a miner from one of the surrounding claims that had back-talked one of Craft's dead men. I didn't blame them for their anger; they deserved to feel the satisfaction that came with killing a man who really needed killing. But Earnest Craft wasn't a man possessed by any sort of reason. If I didn't know better, I would have said that hell itself spat him out, but of course, it had done the same with me.

And I had ways of divining the truth from uncompromising lips.

"Mr. Howe, would you kindly bring the supplies I retrieved?"

My trip topside had been for more than just the Gun. My brief interactions with Earnest Craft had already yielded the immutable knowledge that he was out of his mind. That he would suckle the pain and drink it deep, uncaring that he would die from it. A man who derives pleasure from pain is a tough nut to crack, but by hook or crook, I had the means to pry my desires from him.

Jake came forward, three candles grasped in his right hand, two white and one black. New Orleans had been kind to me last time I'd gone down the bayou way; the coin paid to me had crafted these candles.

The other hand grasped two jars. One contained a fly; hadn't been hard to trap one around here as the insects buzzed all over the place, eager to lap at the blood of dead men. The other contained a black widow spider.

Many a working required sacrifices and symbolism and this one wouldn't be any different. That was the great thing about spiders, they were always hungry.

I went about the beginning, setting candles around Craft and his mother, the black one at the head and the white ones on either side, forming a triangle.

"What's this? Some sort of heathen rite?" Craft laughed but I saw his eyes tracking me as I placed the spider and the fly directly behind the black candle, both jars reflecting the torchlight. The red of the widow seemed to glow in the gloom.

I had an intuition about this man, a feeling that I was pursuing.

The match head flared in my hand, the tiny flame bouncing with life as I sheltered it with my palm. I leaned down to the black candle and spoke as firmly as I could. "This candle represents your lies and the pain you've caused others, the pain you've beseeched unto yourself."

WILE E. YOUNG

Craft waved his hands in the chains, lashing out with his foot to try to knock over the candle; futile, but admirable. "Spooky stuff. I can see why the rubes buy into this."

I moved to the white candles. "Both of these represent the truth and the unlocking of your tongue. Uncovering your deceit and overcoming your will with the eyes of the spirits watching you."

Craft strained at his chains, his mouth twisted in a sneer, eyes boring in me. "You think some redskin magic is going to make me talk? Heard you were a big bad bird, not some greenhorn knocking rocks together trying to scare people."

I smirked at him, but didn't bother to answer. There were rites to observe in a proper working and taking the time to gloat wasn't one of them.

When I reached the head of the triangle, I lifted my head to the cellar ceiling, my eyes tracing the roots dangling through the dirt. "To whatever listens, I offer this smoke as offering. Compel him to release the truth from his blighted tongue." I bent down, unscrewing the lid of the jar holding the fly, swiftly working to trap the insect in the jar with the spider. "Just as the fly is consumed by the spider, I too will consume my enemy. I will drink his insides while he blusters and begs, but no mercy I grant and no relief he'll get."

Black chitinous legs walked lazily across a web that seemed shoddy compared to the elegant things of spiders from the woods, but to a man as invested in death as me, it looked beautiful. Every step towards the struggling fly was a step I mimicked around the triangle of flickering candles. Every buzz of the insect's desperate wings was a shout from Craft and his mother in chains, and every eager snap of the spider's mandibles was a candle blown out, leaving the smoke to drift to the roots above us.

The spider sprang onto the fly, its struggles over quickly.

Craft's were just beginning.

His hands were shaking in his chains now. I drew the Gun and the whispering was practically a laugh in my mind as I aimed it at his head. "Some tribes believe that if you eat a man, you take his power, his soul. Think I'll be doing the same to you. Imagine it, Mr. Craft; an eternity of watching me go about my business. Bit of irony that it's a Comanche ritual that will do you in."

He was sweating now, the working moving under his spirit and loosening the willpower, burning it off into oblivion. There were no threats or bravado now, just the cold panic of a man who'd rather be tortured to death with a hot blade than fall victim to a native rite.

"Goodbye, Mr. Craft. It's been a pleasure." I grinned wickedly, thumbing the hammer back on the Gun.

Craft practically burst forward, his mouth turned down in a sneer and his eyes wide, lips trembling, breathing so fast he could have substituted for a bellows at a fireside. "Alright, you bastard, alright! I'll tell you what you want to know, just don't kill me like this."

And there it was, the yellow belly that men like Earnest Craft had nurtured their entire lives. I grinned; it was a smile that would have silenced birdsong and made babes cry in their sleep. Craft didn't back down from it, he didn't smile or gloat, didn't cry or beg. He just stared at the floor with wide and angry eyes. The man wasn't a coward; the character of his kind didn't have much room for fear, but they had more than enough room to carry hate, and to die by what you hated, that was a poor fate indeed.

"Lamb's a sheriff now. Never had much for him, but when we split ways, I was genuinely happy for his choices. He's gone straight, out in Graverange, exorcising demons from the accounts he settled back in the war."

A sheriff, a lawman; seemed right for the Night Rider. A man could feel guilty about what he'd done if he let the gospel slingers and common decency get to him.

Craft looked at me, twisting his head and grinning. "Word has it the Weber brothers got the invite to be his deputies after a few run-ins out in New Mexico. Those whoremongers are having a good time. Run the saloon pretty good with a few doves. Though last I heard, George ran the place and David stayed properly roostered." He clinked the chains, balling his fists and sighing. "No more chitchat. I'm eager to get on down to hell and watch you come a cropper on those boys."

Could have said that I felt respect for this man. He was going to die more courageous than most, but after everything, the only thing I felt was a cold satisfaction to see it done.

After I had secured the ingredients for the working and retrieved my Gun, I had searched for one more thing, and had found it curled asleep under a dark overhang. It was cooler up here in North Dakota, but the devil's chosen animal was universal in all the places I'd ever laid eyes on.

The rattlesnake was ornery, had been ever since I'd snatched him from under his rock and put him inside the crate where he'd been making his buzzing music ever since.

"A snake? Think I'm afraid of a little snake?" Craft laughed. For a man versed in torture, I was sure that he thought I didn't know dung from wild honey.

"You will be, Mr. Craft, after you see where I'm going to put it. Mr. Howe?"

Jake advanced, the two women whose names I learned were Nellie and Susan following in his footsteps. The two men, Clifton and Joe, held Mrs. Craft still, making sure that she didn't interrupt the death that I was going to bring on her son.

I'd promised Sergeant Craft's victims vengeance, the opportunity to inflict pain on the man who had kidnapped them, humiliated and raped them, marauded his way all across this territory and further beyond. So it did my heart good to hear him scream when Jake shoved the first fishhook through his lower lip. Blood welled up from the wound and he kicked his legs, trying to shove Jake away. My companion held his ground, sweat pouring up around his hair as he tried to hold the man still.

Nellie and Susan shoved the next hook in, making sure that the pointed tip scraped gum as it dug into his cheek. I heard something scraping over the sound of Craft's agony. Dark red blood boiled out of his mouth and spilled out onto the floor.

Mrs. Craft screamed and cursed, reaching out toward her son, but Clifton and Joe kept her firm.

When the last fishhook had wormed its way into his gums, I approached, grasping the head of the snake tight.

"Open wide, Mr. Craft."

Jake pulled hard on the two lines attached to the fishhooks in Craft's lower jaw, while Nellie and Susan pulled on their own respective ones, and the sergeant screamed as his mouth opened wide.

The snake was already striking as I shoved it down his throat. It sank into the man's tongue, the reptile's tail buzzing like a swarm of bees. Craft gurgled, choking on the snake as it found his throat. It'd already bitten his cheek, but I made sure there was only one place for it to go.

The snake's head lodged and bloody foam began to froth between Craft's lips and the scales rubbing against his cheek. Dark veins stood out on his face and his eyes bulged in his head.

I heard him struggling to breathe, the skin in his throat moving and jumping as the snake tried to find its way out. The man gurgled and tried to throw his head only to find more pain as the fishhooks wormed deeper into his gums.

He was close to death now; his chest had stopped moving and his eyes were beginning to slow as they rolled, the whites having turned bloody red as the rattlesnake venom did its work.

I leaned close and whispered into his ear, "You may have practiced bloody craft, but you weren't very imaginative."

There could have been a small laugh in the wheeze

that escaped from between his skin and the snake, then there was nothing. Earnest Craft's body sank in the chains and something pink and foamy dripped to the floor.

His mother sobbed in her chains, repeating the name of her son over and over again, spitting guff and poison at everyone within reach.

"Sirs and madams, Mr. Howe, let's take our leave of this place. Think I've spent as much time as I can handle in this cellar."

They wanted to kill Mrs. Craft, I could see it in their eyes, like hungry wolves eyeing a fresh deer, but after they saw what I had planned... Satisfaction comes in many forms and sometimes just shooting someone is too good for them.

"Take what you can carry if you have want of it, but when I reach the cellar doors, I won't care if you get left behind."

They made their move to leave, but Joe stopped at the yawning darkness and looked back at me warily. "What about the bear?"

I glanced at the coffin, silent, content, like a man who'd just had a good meal and laid down for a siesta in the afternoon sun.

"Wouldn't be worrying about that too much, I expect it had its fill. Now go."

They didn't bother trying to debate any further and, one by one, they filed down the tunnel, footsteps echoing.

"Mr. Howe, take the coffin with you." Jake looked at me. Maybe he saw the weariness there, maybe he didn't, but he didn't complain. He just began to drag my teacher's box away.

I waited until they were gone before I began snuffing the lights from the torches in the room. One by one I began bringing the darkness.

"Going to have your way in the dark? Why don't you just shoot me? Send me off to be with my boy." Mrs. Craft's voice was sullen, despairing.

Good.

"No, Miss Craft, I'm not going to kill you today. I'm not going to kill you at all. The Good Lord provided us ways of dying all our own."

I left her in the dark, screaming for me to kill her, leaving her to the sound of the buzzing rattlesnake trying to free itself from her son's corpse.

Craft's bowie knife was my souvenir; might indulge in a working when I had the time, see all the deaths it had been a part of over the years.

In the dark of the tunnel, I had time to imagine what was in store for Miss Craft. A few days in the blackness listening to the rattlesnake slither across the floor, dying of thirst in the impenetrable gloom as her son's body rotted.

She screamed loud and long as I tossed the dynamite that sealed up the entrance.

CHAPTER SIXTEEN

IT'S BEST TO make tracks after killing any member of the local army element and this time was no different. Craft may have been a son of a bitch and a piece of manure, but he was still army. That wasn't attention I wanted.

Graverange was far. Colorado Territory, nestled up in the mountains with the snow coming in. It would be awfully cold by the time we reached those distant peaks.

The plains were calm this evening. Coyotes yipped in the dark and I leaned against the coach's wheels, reading the stars. Jake sat next to the fire, feet tucked up next to him as he winced, his hand grasping over his shirt that was dark with blood from his injury.

Seen plenty of men lose their nipples over the years; one of the first things you learn when you're in the business of extracting information from the unwilling. Easy to keep from bleeding out, usually by inflicting a bit of further pain. Tends to get your point across quick.

We hadn't spoken much since we left Deadwood, just a few words from him to figure the plan and his place in it. Maybe Miss Holloway's departure was weighing on him, but it wasn't something that I was familiar with, that pain or longing for someone. Sending Virgil off to the Promised Land had cut my ties to anyone that would keep me tethered to my heart.

"Have you looked to that? It'll get infected if you don't."

Jake shook his head, staring into the fire. I could practically see the searing knife cauterizing his chest in my mind, just as it was no doubt playing through his. "I know about soldiering, tracking men, but doctoring wasn't in training. They left that for the sawbones."

A fair assessment and one I smiled at. Jake winced and bit his lip. "Damn. Feels like I took a shot to the chest, it still feels like it's burning."

I chuckled. "It will for a long time. We have a few weeks until we get to Graverange; you'll be right as rain before we get there. I've patched together more than a few in my time."

Jake laughed. It sounded bitter, rough, like water breaking on a rock. "No offense, Salem, but I think you're more gifted in taking the world apart than healing folks."

Wasn't the first time I'd been accused of such, but it'd been a long time since I'd felt what it was like to be stung by them. I didn't bother answering; I just let the Gun whisper comfort to me. More folks needing to be put into the massive hole that festered in my soul. One day, it'd be filled up high and I'd rub the dirt over the top, pat the shovel and come out of the night. Not today, not next year, but maybe someday.

There were a few things I needed in the coach:

herbs I'd picked up over the months, my mortar and pestle, and a consultation with one of my journals. I left the darkness of the stage, already doing my damnedest to crush the plants together in a fine paste.

Jake watched me with interest. "Doesn't look like any medicine I've ever seen."

I spit into the mixture, whispering to it. I felt a smile tug at my lips. "It's not a medicine a white man would ever give you."

His mouth turned into a snarl, but he didn't bother scooting away from me. "If it's all the same, Salem, I'd prefer to try the old style of healing. I don't want any heathen or pagan medicine to touch my—"

"Jake," I said firmly.

My companion's rant stopped mid-sentence. It'd been a long time since I had addressed anyone by their first name; the practice had never sat right with me. It caught Jake's attention and kept it just fine. "From what you've seen, what you've heard, you think I'm a chiseler? Peddling shit and taking lives for the hell of it?"

A pair of tongs lay close by. I clutched the mortar tight in their iron grip and held it over the flame. "When you traveled as much as I have, seen and done things that I've done, you learn that under the skin we're all meat. It just comes in different flavors."

Steam began to drift from the mortar. I brought it close to me, careful not to touch the hot stone, dabbing my fingers into the melted sludge inside and letting the heat shoot through me fast enough to send gooseflesh running through my leathers.

"You've ridden the trail with me hard, you've nearly hanged riding with me, and now you've lost flesh on account of things." I shrugged off my coat, unbuttoning my shirt and letting it fall into the dust.

My back, my chest, my arms, all of it was a tapestry of pain. Gunshots, knife marks, ritualized scarring from all the workings I'd undertaken through the years, more pain than I could rightfully recall.

"Injuries are a testament to a story well written, Mr. Howe. You'll live with this one, and the lesson you can take from it is that your skin isn't any different from those Comanche you so proudly put under the ground."

I gestured for him to remove his shirt and he followed my instructions with trembling hands. The green paste coated my fingers and I reached toward the black and oozing scab where Jake's nipple used to be.

"Think on that while this goes to work." I rubbed it across the rough scab and Jake began screaming as the paste began to burn the infection out of him. His hands jumped to his chest, no doubt to brush off the medicine, but my hands were just as quick, and I held him tight.

"Let it run its course. You'll feel better when it's done." Jake gritted his teeth, the bouncing firelight reflecting off of his eyes as they rolled around, trying to see if there was any relief from the pain.

"Hate to do this to you, but I can't have you dying from infection. I made a promise to you and I aim to keep it."

Jake groaned, the pain causing him to hiss through gritted teeth. I held both of his hands in my grip, firm enough that I was sure I was going to leave bruises.

"Take your mind off of it. The one in Querido, tell me how you met her. Maybe by the time you're done, the hate will be burned out of you."

He spoke of Catarina, how his unit had come down on a few banditos rustling cattle at the border. Jake had snuck off for R&R after the hangings, finding himself over the border and stumbling drunk into a cantina.

An angel, those were the words he used to describe Catarina. If he hadn't been gripping my hands tight enough to squeeze rocks into dirt, I would have laughed. I'd met described angels and none of them had a voice that had turned my heart over.

She'd sang and the patrons had fallen in lust, a few even made to proposition her, but like most things, killing had happened and Jake had found himself with a bloodied knife and the heart of a senorita who sang with the angels. For a man that hated redskins, it was surprising to see him fight so hard for a woman whose skin was brown.

The Federales were going to come, but no one could identify some gringo from across the border, fewer still willing to pursue him. That was how Jake Howe found himself promising a senorita that he would come back, money in his pockets, willing to take her back across to wherever it was that he would end up settling.

"Saw you eyeing Miss Holloway hard when she was with us. Your pole causing you grief enough to turn away from the senorita who sings like an angel?"

Jake was on his back now, face covered in a sheen of sweat, rot and weakness leaving his veins. He smiled up at me and shook his head. "Just being friendly, Salem. Not something you're overly familiar with."

I chuckled. Jake's voice was hoarse and he coughed up spit and green phlegm. His eyes were narrow slits and he sounded weaker than a horse that had gone lame. "Whatever you gave me, Salem, I don't think it's working right. Blasted redskin medicine, it'll kill you."

He said the last bit with a weary laugh that set my temper to blazing anyway. "If I hadn't promised you'd walk away from this, I'd be sending you off to meet the angels themselves."

Jake gripped my hand hard. "Don't give me false hope, Salem. You and I both know there is a bullet waiting at the end of this for me." His head fell back and exhaustion took him, the medicine sapping him of energy.

I stood up and wiped my brow; hadn't realized I'd been sweating either. The next part was going to leave me exhausted, but had to be done.

Retrieving the shovel from the coach, I went about digging the hole I'd bury my companion in.

Jake came to the next morning screaming. His nose barely poked above the soil as he writhed around under the earth. His hand reached up to grasp at the sky like a dead man fresh out of hell.

I sat on a rock close by. I had been watching his nose all night to make sure he continued to draw breath. He struggled out of the dirt and when he saw me, his face turned into a snarl. "You son of a bitch!"

He reached for his piece but only found his empty holster.

I relished the sudden panic in his eyes, could practically see his imagination wondering whether I would draw and send him back down into the dirt, permanent-like this time. Instead I asked him, "How're you feeling?"

Jake's dumfounded expression brought a grin to my weary face. The sun was high in the sky already and it was long since past time that we made tracks. "How am I feeling? You fucking buried me! I ain't like your dead redskin, I'm not going to go about pretending I'm alive from the next life!"

I stood and walked over, offering him a hand. "Pull in your horns and take a look at your chest."

Jake glanced down immediately at the skin, scarred but without a trace of the infected scab where his nipple used to be. The scar stood out against the paleness of his skin, an ugly mess of mottled flesh on his left pectoral that he would carry for the rest of his life.

"What the . . . damn . . . " He couldn't get the words out quite right. Hard thing to fathom when you're first confronted with evidence of real power in the world. Sitting in the hole, he couldn't find the words, finally settling on, "That's . . . that's a hell of a trick."

He reached out and took my hand and I pointed toward the reins, Soldier and Maestro waiting impatiently. "You can chew on that for the rest of the day. I've spent the night making sure you didn't die in that hole and I'm overdue for some rest."

I helped him gather camp, wearily heaving myself

into the darkness of the coach when I was done, calling out before I shut the door, "Stay on the trail to Graverange and wake me if we run into any trouble."

I'd only barely managed to remove my shirt and hat when I felt us begin to move, letting the whisperings of the Gun carry me off into that vast nothingness that felt more peaceful than the sunlit reality I otherwise called home.

CHAPTER SEVENTEEN

WE WERE NEARLY across Nebraska before Jake asked me the question that I was sure had been on his mind since Littlecreek. "Is it true? What they say about you and that Gun?" He pointed at the weapon on my hip and it took everything I had not to cradle it like it was my child.

He'd heard me proclaim the truth plenty, but I hadn't an urge to sit down and speak about the circumstances of my life. That was a story that was known to only one person amongst the living and they weren't from this world.

"You don't need me to go laying things out for you, Mr. Howe, you've already made up your mind about what is and isn't true." I let my eyes drift over the area of his shirt that concealed the scarred flesh from his wound. "You've lived a little proof as well."

His hand subconsciously drifted over and scratched idly, his eyes set hard as he stared at the towers of stone that were the Rockies. "It's a hell of a thing, Mr. Covington, hearing the stories and seeing them. Like that bear. I haven't been able to figure out how you managed to swing that. Most of your mumbo jumbo I've seen you work has all been preparation."

The stage rattled as we crossed a stream, halting Jake in his line of inquiry. I hadn't traveled with anyone this long since the war ended. Most of the outfit with Quantrill had learned it was better not to ask questions; death seemed to find those who peered too close. I'd been younger and more eager to prove things. Killing my brother had taught me that everyone else was just meat walking and a knife in the back was a lot harder to see coming than a gun in front of you.

"Read your bible much, Mr. Howe? Attend the gospel mill on the regular?"

Jake looked at me confused, probably wondering how the bible pertained to his question. I'd never had much use for the strung-out platitudes of long-dead prophets, but curiosity was a hell of a thing. I found myself hoping that Jake wouldn't tumble down the hole where he was already teetering on the edge.

"Yeah, Pa used to read to me when I was young'un. I was baptized in the Sabine River. Don't think the Good Lord looks too kindly on whatever it is you do." At least he knew that much. I'd never been asked to teach these things, can't reckon I would've even if I had been asked, but I knew the slippery slope that led to a chase across the vast and open west.

"There's something in there about powers and principalities, invisible worlds that all good Christians are supposed to avoid."

I wasn't one for quoting the scripture, but I could remember that much.

"Did you do that?" He asked.

"I never was a very good church boy, either. So just heed my advice here, Mr. Howe, and don't go asking questions for things that are going to end up with your soul flayed down to the bone and cooked over a flame hotter than a whorehouse on nickel night." I hoped my words would sway him. I wasn't going to teach him regardless, but that didn't mean that there weren't folks out there willing to show him the ropes. I'd found plenty.

It was funny, really; I wondered how much credit trying to keep him from the dark was going to get me when I stood in judgment, especially since I had a lot more killing planned.

"I understand; Jesus is the man I need to tie to, not whatever it is you've got. I'm not going to go on the shoot, but I've got to know, what was that bear?"

Sometimes, even when warned, curiosity and that itch like a horsefly of unanswered questions trumped all caution. I felt the smile dance across my face, felt eyes from something I couldn't see watching me . . . my teacher, wondering what I would say.

"Life and death is a line. If you're skilled enough, strong as hell, and know the way back, you can come back in the form that suits you best. Strong feeling helps, and nothing's stronger than anger and hate. An unjust murder? Nothing breeds hate like that."

His eyes might have been focused on the trail, ruts carved into the mud and grass from all manner of stages and wagons that had come before, but he was all ears, eager like a greenhorn to learn what came next.

"All that hate and anger, it drives you, consumes you. I've plenty of it myself. You tend to lash out as time goes on and you find yourself stuck and unable to pass on, unable to hurt like you've been hurt."

Something thumped on the back of the coach. Most folks would have thought that a rock had been kicked up by the back wheel and thrown against the paneling. Most folks.

"You don't think. You can't shake friend from foe. That kind of anger needs to be bound, kept safe lest you condemn yourself to weariness from now until kingdom come."

Jake's eyes glanced back at the coffin, the chains wound tight around the wood, bouncing and groaning with each turn of the wheel. He was beginning to understand just why I had respect for my teacher, even in death.

Time to four flush him and kill that curiosity. Safer that way. "Of course, sometimes when there is loads of meat just waiting to be picked, a bear is just a bear."

Jake looked at me like he'd been kicked in the rear by a mule, then slowly shook his head. "You like being a flannel mouth, don't you, Mr. Covington?"

A sign hung from a stone, 'Leaving Nebraska' etched into it. We had finally made it to the Colorado Territory.

"Only because I don't have many people eager to speak with me, Mr. Howe. I've usually killed them by now."

CHAPTER EIGHTEEN

THUNDER **RUMBLED THROUGH** the mountains as we overlooked Graverange. It was a modest thing; the snowfall had come early, and through fading sunlight the town looked like a refuge from the elements. Orange lights twinkled in the valley below, several homesteads spread out before us.

The winter looked like it brought peace over this place. Shame that I was going to end that.

I didn't expect this to be like the others. The Weber brothers and August Lamb had made themselves public figures, probably beloved by their towns. There wouldn't be any bushwhacking or outright murder here. This would require guile and the ability to outrun a posse. A gun might not have been able to kill me, but a noose and the appropriate amount of fists sure would do the trick.

"What's your plan? Storm the town, kill everyone who raises a gun? Not all of these people killed your redskin." Jake stood in the snow, shivering under the skinned wolf pelt I'd given him to keep warm. His words irritated me; we'd been civil in our trip across the plains and I did admit that I had taken a shine to the man, if only for him being alive around me longer than most people I knew.

Storming the town had been the first option, but it wasn't my fault that they had decided to elect a murderer as their sheriff.

I would have his blood.

"While the decimation of some fur town on the edge of nowhere does intrigue me, we have enough to deal with without the entire territory coming after us."

Jake gestured for the binoculars and I handed them over so that he could read the situation and come to his own conclusions.

I had something more explosive in mind.

The dynamite fit easily into the snow. Jake ran the fuses to the plunger, his fingers red and trembling in the cold air. "What happens if they're having a bad year? Foul crop or a whole mess of dead livestock? You'll be condemning them to starve."

"You've ridden the trail with me for a while now, Mr. Howe. The problems of these people aren't something I care about. Death comes for everyone, by bullet or time. This just keeps me from sending them to meet their maker early."

We finished the work and saddled Soldier and Maestro. Jake looked sick at his stomach, his hands trembling, and it looked like he might've been sweating despite the cold.

"Something troubling you?"

Soldier stamped the ground and Jake's hands grasped the saddle horn like he was afraid the animal would buck him off. "This isn't like Craft or Maddox; this is a lawman. The few times I saw him at Fort Sill, he didn't seem like the sergeant . . . "

It was almost like he was trying to sway me, as if I'd killed enough people, that vengeance would be carried out by God and to leave it at that.

I wasn't near close to done.

"He's a good man, Salem. Let him go."

"I appreciate your opinion, Mr. Howe. You have three men to identify, then you'll earn your gold."

Jake settled back in the saddle, nodding his head once. "That's the way it is, then. At least when they hang me, I won't be feeling guilty about it."

I chuckled and urged Maestro forward, calling back behind me. "They won't be hanging you for taking the French leave if you're living in Mexico, bag of gold in hand and your pole buried deep in that senorita."

Highhandedness tended to disappear when you reminded them of the escape they could have, dangling that carrot to tempt them forward. Jake was no exception and I heard Soldier's hooves begin to tramp through the snow as we descended into the valley.

There was a stable to the south, the Weber brothers' saloon squatted in the middle of the town with the general store across the street from it, a butcher shop, looked like a gunsmith, and a church behind it all, the local boot hill surrounding it in circles of marble.

I spotted the hanging sheriff sign and steered

clear. I knew where to find the Night Rider when the time came, but the Weber brothers were another matter. They could have been anyone in this town. I was sure that Jake would full on try to kill me if I just chose townsfolk at random.

Eyes watched us as we rode into town, flickers of fire from pipes and lit cigarettes in the shadows, tiny pinpricks of orange. Been riding long enough that I knew when I was being watched, side effect of strangers; or were we expected?

My hand drifted to the Gun nonetheless, the whispers almost overpowering, urging me not to listen to Jake's inane naiveite, let the whole damn country know what happened when they killed someone you respected. I whispered back to the weapon, letting it know that it would be able to drink its blood soon enough.

We hitched the horses outside the saloon. Jake blew on his hands but mine never left the inside of my coat; I wasn't aiming to let my guard down now that I was in the middle of my enemy's land.

It seemed like folks had come in from their homesteads; laughter, music, and the clank of mugs against the bar rang out of the saloon. We reached the door and I gestured for Jake to enter first, eager to shield him in case someone decided that shooting us in the back was worth a lifetime of their friends accusing them of cowardice.

A few heads turned when we walked in. There were a few shouts to close the door, what little warmth there was seeping out as we stood there in the entry.

"To the bar, nice and easy. We don't want to start

a war, not yet." My whisper reached Jake's ears as we moved forward, spurs clicking against the wooden floor, but no one paid us any mind. Wasn't natural; small town like this, heads should have been turning every few seconds to take a look at the newcomers. My hand, already gripped around my weapon, gripped tighter, and the whispers told me that everyone in this room wanted my neck in a noose.

I wouldn't swing, not today.

The bartender had a long face with a small moustache dusting his lip, a stained red vest, scarlet cheeks from the cold, and his breath coming out in small wisps of mist. "Evening, gentleman. Welcome to Graverange."

I tipped my hat to him as I took a seat. Jake offered a smile as he took the stool next to me. "It's been a cold time, barkeep. Hope you have something warmer than the regular piss we've been drinking across the prairie?"

The bartender chuckled. "Everyone's looking for the good stuff, mister. Can't say whether it'll meet your fancy palate or not, but I'm sure willing to give it a go. As long as you can pay?"

The coins clinked onto the bar. The man scooped them up eagerly and I heard him begin to work the tap as he poured our beers.

My eyes never left the tables; men drinking and playing cards, a poker game in the corner, other conversations as they relaxed after a long day of work or just wanted to escape from their families for a night at the saloon. Tension covered the room, more than the regular amount of tension that came with playing hands with folks who'd kill you over a slipped ace.

Jake nudged my arm and slid the beer into my grasp. I took a few sips but didn't allow myself a long draft; you didn't celebrate in the middle of the wolves' den.

A few working women lined the stairs, fans waving like they were in some big burg back east, dollied and painted up well enough that an entirely different hunger gnawed at my mind that had nothing to do with killing. That sweetheart in Furnace had been months ago. A man could use a good filly every now and again, and I had more than enough coin to pay.

Maybe when this was over.

"Don't get too roostered on your drink, Mr. Howe. I can't have you seeing double."

Jake took another sip of his beer and motioned with his head toward the stairs. "No need to get your union suit bunched up. There goes the first one."

A man stumbled down the stairs, a dove in a burgundy corset and not much else supporting him. He laughed and staggered, jet-black hair falling over his face that dripped sweat.

It was my first look at the older Weber brother, and I wasn't impressed. If the lady hadn't bothered to stick him back in his flannel and work pants, wet with melted snow, I was sure that he would have stumbled down those stares as naked as the day he came out of his mama. He stumbled when he got to the bottom of the stairs, reaching out and grabbing the bannister for support. His deputy star gleamed as he laughed uproariously, swaggering to his full height, a bottle of gin clasped firmly in his hand.

"Big falls, big drinks, everyone gets a round on the house!"

A round of cheers went up around the saloon, but no one moved to take him up on his offer. Seeing the bartender duck into a doorway behind me, I figured this must've been a well-known routine, the sauced co-owner promising things that his brother probably didn't intend on granting.

"That's David, there's the other one, right on cue." Jake pointed at a man who emerged from somewhere deeper in the saloon. George "Sly Eye" Weber was thicker set with dark black pants and suspenders stretching across his deep navy shirt.

He shook his head as he went over to grab his brother. "Come on, David. Let's have you sleep it off."

David Weber waved a hand at his brother. "Get away from me, damn you. I'm enjoying a fine refreshing drip of . . . of . . . " His eyes went blank as his lips puckered and sucked at air like a fish flopping on land trying to breathe. He suddenly smiled and looked at his brother like he had just heard he'd retire like the swells with the biggest score this side of a train job. "A drip of our fine vintage!"

He took another long swig as the woman he had walked downstairs with leaned over the bannister, cleavage strewn right in her boss's face. "I tried to keep it out of his hands, Georgie boy, but his paws were all over me and the drink."

George took off his grey union cap, running a hand through his matching hair. "Thank you, Lilah. I'll see him home. You can head back to work."

She ran a gloved hand across his palm, giving him a wink of an eye. "You work too hard, deputy. Why don't you come around more often and I'll give you a free roll . . . keep the spry in your bones a bit longer."

George grinned and gave a small shake of his head, looking at his brother liquored up and assbound at the foot of the stairs. "When this one comes to and Sheriff Lamb has him out guarding the pass for those fellows, I might take you up on that."

She gave a teasing, pouting face. "Don't keep me waiting too long." The dove walked toward the poker game, eager to ease some john out of his winnings, but my mind was only focused on George and his brother.

"What are you thinking, do we wait for Lamb?"

Jake may not have noticed, but George Weber's words stuck with me. 'Those fellows'. They knew we were coming, word had traveled across the prairie about Maddox and Craft . . . Or we had been sold out, euchred before we ever got started.

It wasn't a distrust of newcomers I'd felt, it was the deep breath before you drew iron. Every man in here knew who we were. All of them were probably ready to draw and send Jake hurtling to the Promised Land.

So why hadn't they?

"No, Mr. Howe, not this time. I'm going to say you fulfilled your word."

I didn't have the gold on me; I had planned on paying him after we were a long way from here, but as it stood, I wondered if I'd be making it out alive myself. Needs must when the devil drives and he'd been driving me for a long time.

"What do you mean? This whole town is going to be on you. They'll have you swinging before the sun is up."

Most of this town was going to be dead by sun up,

and if I swung, it would be because the Webers and Lamb were dead.

"Go back to the coach. Take it down to Galveston and look for a man named Lonesome Cole; he'll pay you a good price for all of it. The gold I've promised you is in the chest beneath my teacher's coffin. Take that for the service you've given me."

A figure appeared at the stairs. My eyes hardened when I saw her, dressed in a deep emerald with her hair done up in thick curls. The dress matched her eyes which stared at me with a viper's gaze.

Jake followed my stare and saw Ruby Holloway grasping the bannister with her fingernails.

The men around the saloon stood up, pistol hammers clicking back beneath their coats as the ladies who had been entertaining them scurried off to safer environs. The Weber brothers both emerged from the back of the saloon, David wearing a shit eating grin and remarkably less drunk than he had seemed. George "Sly Eye" had a rolling block rifle aimed directly at Jake's head. I imagined that all of them were aimed at my companion.

"You bitch! You sold us out!"

Ruby's eyes were hard, but she shook her head. "Not you, Jake. Just him." Her voice dripped with enough venom that I couldn't rightly reckon if she wasn't a serpent who had taken human form.

I tipped my hat to her, but any retort I might have given was cut off by the sounds of heavy boot falls. The men in the saloon turned to look up as a man stepped into view next to Ruby. He was cadaverously thin, looked like a stick bug that had learned how to walk on two legs. His black hat was rugged and pitted, his cheeks sunken beneath it like a bare skull that someone had only put skin on as an afterthought, and his chin was covered in dark hair marred only by two long scars.

Thrown over his shoulders was a skin of white fur, covered with strange designs that would have hurt the eyes of any regular trail man that looked. I knew the fur of the white bison, the skin of the animal that my teacher had died for. And I knew that this man was August Lamb, the Night Rider.

"Welcome to Graverange, gentlemen. We've been expecting you for weeks."

I stood and watched the pistols come from under the men's coats, all of them clicking and ready to put a bullet in me. August Lamb raised his hands, "Easy now, men, easy. You've all heard the stories same as me."

He walked past Ruby, and I thought I saw her shiver as he passed. The cadaverous sheriff made the motion of a gun with his left hand as he descended the stairs. "The Black Magpie, man killer, burner of homes, collector of lives, he can't be killed by a gun."

All true, but I wasn't eager to go about proving it, if only because I had made promises to Jake that he would walk away from this. With the number of guns pointing our way, he wouldn't make it two steps before he was business for the local undertaker.

I rested easily at the bar, my back leaning against the wood paneling, more than sure that the bartender was aiming a sawed off at my back. I tried to pay it no mind. I'd been looking forward to meeting this man. "I see you've been casting an ear for my story, Sheriff. I've heard yours too, but I'm eager to learn the little bits of it you haven't told your good townsfolk here."

The men shuffled uneasily and the jackal smile disappeared from his face and was replaced with a cold glare. He looked over at Jake. "Private Howe, Ruby tells me that you've been held hostage and coerced by this man. Not to say that ain't a hanging offense, but she tells me that you're a good fellow. I'm inclined to agree, seeing as you were with us when we killed those savages back in Oklahoma. I want you to step away from Mr. Covington, and I'll make sure that the army won't find you here."

It was a good offer, seeing as how I'd already gone and told Jake where the gold was located. Tempting deal for a good man and unthinkable for an honorable one, but for a man like me it was the only choice that would have made sense. Could see Jake contemplating it, his hand falling away from his gun. "I don't . . ."

I wrapped one arm around his neck and pressed my Gun to his temple. "I don't think that you need to finish that thought, Mr. Howe."

Every man in the building's gun was on me and I heard the bartender cock his shotgun behind me. August Lamb held up both of his hands. "Hold your fire, boys, hold your fire. Let Mr. Covington figure out there isn't a way out of this. We've got him dead to rights."

Couldn't deny him that. If the men rushed me now, I'd be able to kill a few of them, but not enough. I'd be hogtied on the floor and ready to meet the noose before I could kill those I'd came for.

"You—you said I'd walk away," Jake coughed around the tight grip I held on his throat. He was sweating profusely and my Gun lapped up the salty liquid and eagerly whispered for me to kill him. But I wouldn't do that, not yet. He hadn't betrayed me in word or deed, and I was a man who honored his agreements.

"You will walk away, just had to make sure you weren't going to go and take a better offer."

I thought I felt Jake trying to laugh between his desperate breaths. "The only person who does whatever they want . . . is you." An accurate assessment, but I was long past guilt.

"Don't think I'm licked yet, Sheriff. Believe I'm going to be dancing merry on top of your graves before this is all said and done with."

George "Sly Eye" Weber pointed the rolling block at my head. One bullet from that could make a man look like he was nothing but a pile of blood, shit, and meat. "I've got him dead to rights, boss. I can pulp him easy without harming a hair on the poor little private's head."

Didn't doubt the marksman's claim, and any other day I would have been eager to see him try, but the crowd was restless; one shot and they'd mob us. My mind drifted to a snow-covered ridge, not far from here, where my teacher lay in his coffin and the dynamite I had planted in the snow sat waiting. I'd never reached out this far before, but I didn't have any choice. It was that or sacrifice Jake for a killing shot.

The words whispered out of me and I saw Jake begin to turn pale. I shut my eyes and heard Lamb speak from far away, "Save the praying, Mr. Covington. You've done just about every crime and sin under the sun."

If only he knew that I still had plenty more sins to commit.

I could see it in my mind: the plunger sitting next to my coach, wind blowing snow across the wood and wire. Slowly, it started to descend.

I opened my eyes again and smiled at Lamb. His hand immediately reached for his gun, eyes narrowing as he tried to work out what I was planning.

"I know your story, Sheriff. I know about Andersonville, the hunger. Have you been that hungry since? I bet you haven't. I bet you've eaten well, as much has you can without feeling guilt. I wonder how you'll fare through the winter without a way to get new supplies?"

David jabbed his gun towards me. "What're you—"

In the mountains, the plunger I'd spelled into motion finally dropped and the dynamite resting comfortably in the snow detonated. Echoing booms ran down the valley and then there was a deep rumble that seemed to go on and on. I'd placed the charges well; the pass would be completely blocked.

Lamb's face went pale, and inside me, something dark ate the expression with a joyous roar.

I pushed Jake forward and shot the nearest man. Grey bits of brain matter splashed over Lamb's face as I rolled behind the bar and took the bartender with me. My Gun blazed and the bartender's dying scream became a bubbling splash as the back of his throat disappeared.

Tables upended and I heard Lamb shouting orders. A few gunshots flew but I paid no mind. The sawn-off felt good in my hand as I rose.

One man had been eager to investigate and as I rose, the shotgun found his face. There was a roar like miniature thunder and I saw the man's face disappear in a sudden flash of fire and buckshot. There was wet squelch, bits of bone, hair, and blood splattering as his body fell to the floor, hands still twitching.

Jake was being ushered to the stairs by George Weber. David had finally gotten a handle on the panicking townsfolk and iron had begun to speak, bottles of hooch shattering behind me as new holes in the wall were created.

I stood full, firing with my Gun and the sawed off into the crowd, most of them diving for cover except for Lamb.

The sheriff raised his Gun and I felt my mind go silent. The weapon fired and the bullet tore into my shoulder. I felt something warm there and I looked to see my own blood pooling beneath my coat.

He fired again. It caught me in the guts and I stumbled backward, glass slicing at me as I fell through the window and into the cold winter snow. I wheezed pitifully like a dog that had been kicked in its side. I left the sawed off and clutched my Gun tight, dragging myself away. It wasn't whispering, there was no eagerness now, but I could hear it panicking, whimpering, begging me to run.

Get it together; you're not an ordinary man. You've killed much and have much more to do. You can't die face down in the snow like a dog.

Except I could. It seemed fitting; my story would end because I hadn't prepared or thought that any of my quarry could be the means of my end.

But that's the way it was. I couldn't be brought

down by a gun; only a bullet from the Brother Guns could kill me.

And August Lamb had the other one.

CHAPTER NINETEEN

WASN'T ENTIRELY SURE how I made it back. The trees and the snow all seemed to blur together over distant shouts and the baying of hunting dogs. I was dying an inch at a time, my blood left behind me in a long trail that only stopped when I reached the ridge overlooking Graverange.

Two bullets burned, one in my shoulder and another in my guts just below my ribs. It was that one that worried me the most; I was a dead man if my innards were bleeding into my belly.

I felt weak; my legs barely kept me standing and I didn't feel the cold anymore. My heart was slow to beat as I mounted the last few steps that would lead to the clearing overlooking the pass.

The pass was gone; a huge avalanche of snow covered the mountainside and my stage was buried halfway to the door on its side, one brown wheel sticking above the powder.

Part of me hoped that the coach would survive. I'd spent years with it and all of the possessions decorating its interior. My plan had been to seal the pass after we'd killed the three men, cut off any pursuit.

THE MAGPIE COFFIN

To say things had gone sideways was an understatement.

A few dead trees had been shaken loose from their roots by the tide of snow and I let my legs give out when I was near enough that I could lean back and rest comfortably, trying hard to keep breathing and wincing as I cupped the wound in my guts. I wanted to close my eyes, even with the Gun screaming in my mind to stay awake, to keep going.

Been riding the trail for a long time and all I wanted was to kill the sons of bitches who did me in and rest easy. Looks like I'd be experiencing one of those things sooner than the other one.

Darkness took me and when I smelled the burnt odor of logs and the quick crackling of flames, I was sure that I'd gone off into that old inferno that had been prepared for me. I reached for my Gun only to find it missing. Supposed that made sense; Old Scratch wouldn't have me defending myself from all the red delights no doubt planned for me.

Then I felt the cold, soaking through my pants and caressing my skin. I opened bleary eyes only to see the snow, the darkness of the night, and a fire burning near me.

Dead Bear sat on a log opposite me. He held the Gun in his hands, fiddling with the hammer. I moaned and reached a trembling hand for it. The dead shaman made no move to give it to me, his black eyes regarding me like a deer struggling to breathe after the arrow entered its neck.

I strained to turn my head, trying to confirm what I already knew. The coffin lay close to the buried coach; the chains had broken from it and my teacher's body was gone. He was free to roam the world and take his vengeance, no doubt starting with me.

I chuckled and leaned back to stare at the stars. "You've only got three left, teacher. Best get to it before they come looking to carry you fully to the other side."

Wasn't expecting mercy, so when the dead shaman rose, I expected to find the Gun pointing at my head or bear jaws wrapping around my face to wring the life from me. I closed my eyes and waited for the inevitable, but it never came.

Hands pressed into my chest and then I felt the burning. Dead Bear worked his way into my guts, and each movement of his fingers brought a wave of fresh agony. It was like heated metal pressing into my flesh. I howled into the night and Dead Bear threw back his head to join me. Somewhere down in the valley, nursing mothers felt a chill run down their spines, wondering what could have made such an unholy sound.

The snow sizzled under me and I watched as Dead Bear retracted his hand and held the dented and misshapen bullet in his hands. He whispered things that made the stars seem to retreat from the heavens and leave just the two of us on that ridge, a fire crackling. Molten metal ran from his head, little grey rivers dripping down and melting the snow as he approached me again, reaching for my shoulder.

I coughed and tried to wave him off, but his hand shot out quick and for a blink of the eye, his feature's peeled away to reveal a bear skull, chunks of flesh hanging from his teeth. The bear skull spoke and my teacher's voice came from it. "You're already halfway over; if I don't remove these, you'll die."

It hurt to laugh, but I waved him away. "Thought you'd want to see that, since I still owe thousands more."

"Whatever pact you made is on your spirit, but these men are bad. They'll kill the one who has traveled with you. You've driven the Lamb to it; you recalled his time in the hunger, reminded him of what he did not to starve. Even now he carves the knives to take the flesh from your friend."

I breathed deep; trying to swallow cold air like it would soothe the searing ache in my guts. I glowered at my teacher, refusing to accept the implication. "I did this to keep them from following us. He wasn't supposed to have the other Gun."

Dead Bear's hands shot into my shoulder, breaking through bone and widening the flesh as he dug to the bullet. Even through the agony, I heard his words.

"You did it because you're a savage. You wanted to pay your debt and condemn them to starve for the winter. Now you want to run, don't try to deny it. I can see it written on your face. That's what you were trying to do coming back here. You were hoping you could escape."

He pushed off with one hand, leaving a burn in the shape of a paw print on my shoulder, the second bullet clutched firmly in his grip. "I've let you take your vengeance for me. I've followed you, and even after you wake up, I'll still go with you. You must decide whether you're willing to look death in the face, and be unafraid, just as you've always claimed."

I faded, but Dead Bear clutched my face tight. "Or have you always been a coward?"

A wetness tickled my skin and I felt my arms being pulled, dragging me from leaning against the log. There were happy yips and growls, bits of pressure on the material of my coat. Pain shot through me as something sharp bit into my shoulder.

I opened my eyes and found four coyotes eagerly attempting to make a meal of me. The largest one's teeth had pierced into my shoulder and I could see his tongue greedily licking at my wound, drinking my blood as it steamed into the night air. I roared and grabbed the animal by its scruff, flinging it into the snow. The animal bounced once and rolled, yipping and whining, before it came to a stop. Its compatriots retreated, but not far enough that I couldn't hear their low growling.

I clawed at my wounds, but I couldn't feel their pain. Whatever Dead Bear had done had taken it from me.

I built a fire as best I could, my lame arm holding my sore stomach as I stacked the logs. The flame danced and drove the darkness back, revealing coyote eyes gleaming in the dark, hoping that I'd take the long one and they'd find an easy meal.

Coward . . . I wasn't a coward, at least I had never styled myself as one.

I'd collect him soon enough.

Until then, I howled and let my war cry sound through the trees, letting the people know . . .

I was coming for them.

CHAPTER TWENTY

THE COFFIN DRAGGED behind me, digging a rut through the snow. It wouldn't be long now.

Coyotes yipped and darted through the trees around me. My conjuring had worked well and they followed the scent of my blood.

Lanterns lit the trees ahead and I heard the nickering of horses as they fought their way through the snow. I faded into the darkness and let the limbs of an evergreen wrap me up.

"You sure it was this way?" It was a voice I didn't recognize. By my reckoning there were at least five of them. I tapped the edge of my holster, wondering if these men were worth killing.

"The Douglass' heard his screaming from up here. With the two bullets Sheriff put in him, he shouldn't be a problem, gun or no gun." That was a voice I recognized. After all, I'd come here to kill him.

"Sly Eye" Weber sat atop his horse, rifle scanning the tree line for anything, and settling exactly on what I wanted him to find. "Bosco, there's something up there; between that rock and the pine, looks like a big box."

Set the trap, wait for the rats.

I heard the man, Bosco, grumble as his boots hit the snow, powder crunching under his heels as he made his way up the hill.

The working felt warm in my hand. I'd squeezed my blood into it and I could smell that warm metal scent. More importantly, so could the coyotes.

Bosco reached the summit, an arm's length from me sitting in the darkness beneath the pine.

"It's a coffin, boss!"

I whispered the final little words, letting the magic do its work and I tossed the small cloth sack of flesh and blood toward the horses.

"What the—" George Weber barely had time to be confused before the yipping and howling began. Coyotes, a dozen of them, ran between the trees and rocks, eager to get at the bloody working I had crafted for them. A few of the men tried to hit the darting animals, their horses barely under control. Bosco tried to run back down the hill to help, but I stepped from behind the trees and drew him back into the dark, slicing his throat as I went. He didn't last long; he'd already been breathing hard and his blood splashed into the snow like a water wagon that had sprung a leak.

I leaned out from behind the tree and took careful aim. My Gun spoke and their horses went down. A few men hollered as five hundred pounds of flesh fell on them. George rolled and brought his rifle up, immediately scanning to see where the shots had come from.

"Covington? Come on out now! You got the drop, but you can't kill all of us."

I eased through the shadows, circling around

them like a hawk watching mice. A twig snapped and George turned, his sly eye aiming down the barrel, his men calling for help from under the weight of their dead horses. He was looking at something in the shadows to my left. I let the evergreens cover me. I was only moving at half speed; the bullets from my brother's Gun had taken their toll on my flesh and my soul.

"You can't win this, Covington, I'll see you coming and send you right on down to hell!"

I had no doubt he would see me. That 'sly eye' of his was notorious throughout the territory, but he'd miss all the same. It was him and his other men struggling out from beneath the dead nags; together they could rush me before I killed them. That's why I had set up a distraction.

I threw my voice, letting the wind carry it to where I needed it to go. "The rest of you, put down your weapons and leave. George Weber is the only one I want. You three can live."

Weber swept his rifle in the direction of my voice. He aimed down the sight and I eased closer, moving silently through the snowbanks.

The sharpshooter smiled as he spied what he thought was me under a tree. "Don't listen to him, boys. We've got him licked. He's just a man; Sheriff already proved that!"

I smirked as he fired. The bullet flew and blood splattered into the snow as Bosco's body toppled out of the trees where I had propped him. He might have looked a sight: mouth hanging open like a dead fish, neck sliced deep enough that you could see the bone and severed muscle.

Weber had the blink of an eye to realize his mistake, then I was among them, my Gun taking the lives of each of his three men in quick succession, bullets finding their way into their hearts and heads.

Blood ran and George tried to swing his rifle to fire at me. I fired on instinct and George screamed as his trigger and middle finger disappeared. Small flaps of skin ran red as he fell back into the snow, flailing and doing his damndest to hold onto the rifle. Even through his tear-stained eyes I could see him trying to wrap his thumb through to pull the trigger.

"That's enough of that." I reached down and pulled the rifle from his maimed hand and he fell back into the snow, gnashing his teeth and grabbing the snow like it was a blanket he could pull over himself to hide from the monster.

"Damn you! Damn you, you bastard!"

I put a finger to my lips and winced as I squatted next to the man, my cauterized wounds protesting.

"Tell me, George Weber, what did you do when you killed my teacher?"

The man spit onto the ground, snot running out of his nose, getting caught in his moustache. "I shot his fucking cow, the white one, right through the head. Felt good to watch him cry over the damn thing. Then he went and threatened us with you."

George chuckled as he massaged his missing fingers, groaning as his remaining hand passed over the ragged bones and torn strips of flesh barely hanging to the rest of his hand. "Guess we should have taken that to heart. Fuck this hurts bad."

"Don't worry," I replied raising my gun. "It won't hurt for long." I hit him hard across the head, watching his eyes roll back as he toppled into the snow.

Coyotes yipped in the night and all was silent.

I went about my work as efficiently as possible; easier than most times since George slept the undisturbed sleep of a man who thought he'd rise up to the Good Lord in that unfeeling black, but it wasn't going to be that easy for him. My knife was kept hot; cauterizing the wounds that would kill him before he woke and letting the others run and stain the snow.

The coyotes came close, darting forward to claim bits of flesh from the dead men and horses. I ignored them, letting them have their fill. When my work was done, I sat back and waited.

The eldest Weber brother came to with a pained scream that sounded like a toad croaking. I smiled as I regarded the ruin that used to be a man. "Welcome back, Mr. Weber. I was hoping that you hadn't bled out."

"What have you done to me?" He asked, though it came out as little more than panicked grunting and groaning. I'd cut out his tongue.

I held the still warm organ in my hand, letting it flop between my fingers. "I couldn't have you calling for help or begging. I would apologize, but this was coming for you from the day you killed that buffalo."

If he had been whole, he would have seethed with rage, but as it was now, he cried tears of panic. They merged with the blood running out of the dark holes where I had torn out his eyes.

He shivered in the cold, the nubs of his fingers desperately trying to wrap around his naked body. I'd taken his clothes from him as well as his fingers. I wore them around my neck. Anticipation came as I imagined what David Weber would do when he saw his brother's digits now as decoration.

George screamed something that was probably a curse. He flailed and fell into the snow, screaming as the burnt flesh found the cold.

"Not gonna kill you, Mr. Weber; I'm going to leave you here amongst the pretty white snow, see if you can find your way back to town. Maybe you can. I won't kill you there if I see you. Maybe you're the strong one between you and your brother. I intend to call on him next."

I stood up and George Weber screamed incomprehensibly, standing and walking toward where he thought I was, stumbling and falling into the snow with a deep whine.

Shouldn't have killed all the horses; would've saved time, but I wasn't opposed to walking.

"I'd hurry if I were you; man in your condition, you've got a fight on two fronts . . . " The ravenous coyotes began to creep from the woods, watching the stumbling man as he tripped and fell against a tree, worthless hands trying to grasp the wood.

"Cold or coyotes, Mr. Weber. Enjoy your life." Grabbing the chain of Dead Bear's coffin, I walked down the mountain as George Weber screamed behind me.

CHAPTER TWENTY-ONE

"THEY HAVEN'T COME BACK."
David Weber fidgeted in his chair, lantern light playing over his features as he squeezed underneath the whore's dress.

August Lamb stared impassively out the window. I wondered if his Gun whispered to him that I was outside, watching them from the dark. Below the window, I waited and I listened.

"If your brother died, would it really bother you?"

I could imagine the smile playing across his lips as he bit lightly into his woman's shoulder. "I'd inherit the saloon, run it like I want. Wouldn't have to pay for tail anymore."

"That's all you've ever done since we signed up: chase tail. Even when we were killing Injuns."

I heard the chair slide back; David must've stood up. "A hog killing good time, but I prefer the warm comforts of a woman's cock trap." The Weber brother laughed at his vulgarity. Lamb did not.

"You ever been hungry, David? Really hungry? Where you lay awake in the night and your stomach is twisted so tight you can't even swallow your own spit because your body is eating you?" Lamb sighed and I knew he was staring out at the collapsed pass. "Won't get any caravans or traders until spring and we don't have enough livestock to slaughter."

"So what? A couple of us will trek over the pass, get on over to Rich Post, and pick up some meat as it comes. It's not as bad as you think."

It was useless to explain to Weber that Lamb's mind was still reliving his time in the war, and what he had done to survive it.

"You could do that, you could die doing it, but you didn't answer my question, which is good enough. You've indulged your appetites, but you've never gone without." I saw the shadow move away from the window, but I heard him state his intent just the same. "Luckily, his partner will get us through until we can get over the pass."

"You can't be serious? That's some shit that the sergeant would do, August. I like flesh but only if I'm dipping my pecker into it, I leave it at that."

Thought I heard Lamb chuckle. "Men used to say the same thing back in Andersonville, wouldn't eat what I brought. No offense taken; if I hadn't been starving, I would have done the same." I heard him grunt heavily. "When they were rail thin and woke to rats gnawing on them in the night, then they begged me to do the night runs. You'll get there too before long."

David Weber was silent for once.

"Get on over to the saloon and round up a few men, teams of two. Get them in spots around town and maybe we can spot him coming."

I'm already here Lamb, but I appreciate you sending my quarry out from your presence. Gives me more time to work something awful on him.

"Don't show your bones yet, boss. George could've killed him, could be riding back down right now with Covington's head."

The door to the Sheriff's office opened and Lamb patted Weber on the back. "More likely he's coming down with your brother's head. Now go."

David didn't protest. He walked arm in arm with the woman, both of them hurrying to get out of the snow.

I watched from the shadow of the building; thought about taking the shot if I wasn't sure that Lamb would be on me. One shot and I would be shuffled off to boot hill.

Too many guns in this town, and with my bum arm and my gut still spitting fire, I'd be hard-pressed to kill them all without scoring a shot from Lamb. I needed a distraction, something with mojo. Needed to rescue Jake too, wherever he was. He'd saved my life, hated to ask him for more, but necessity compels, and I had a mighty need this winter night.

I'd left Dead Bear's coffin amongst a copse of pines right on the edge of the settlement. The evergreens grew thick and I could smell the fresh scents from the trees as I entered. I sat in the snow, feeling the cold shoot through my pants as I pulled my knees to me, staring at the coffin.

"Don't know if you can hear me, I'm assuming you can. Don't know how much power you used up healing me back up at the pass, but I'm close now. These sons of bitches will wish they hadn't killed you by the time I'm done with them."

Took a deep breath. I would have rather done anything than ask more of my teacher, if only for my pride. I was used to coming out on top after any dust up; wasn't used to feeling fear before I walked into a fight.

"I need your help. There's at least a dozen guns in this town, plus Lamb, and I'm not eager to shuffle off just yet. I know that Virgil and I perverted your teachings, same with Stoltzfus and the Robichaudes, and you know that I'd rather put one right in my head than ask for help or admit I was wrong."

Felt good really to unburden and untangle those parts of your soul that you didn't admit to. You travel around thinking you're the worst hombre long enough and you might actually start to believe it.

Tell you the truth, we're just walking dead men on our way to oblivion, Gun or not.

"But if you have the mojo, and the inclination, I could use the help. Just like you did with Craft."

The coffin was silent, the wind still, like the noise of the territory had been turned off and replaced by a quiet void.

"Didn't expect much, just thought I'd ask. I'll give it my all, go out with my boots on, hopefully save Jake while I'm at it. Maybe I'll collect more stories before I stand in front of the devil."

I tipped my hat to the coffin and my teacher. If I didn't come back, the snow would bury it. They'd find him in the spring, but hopefully his soul would have long since departed.

"See you on the other side, teacher."

I put away those things that made me soft and clothed myself in the spirit of the outlaw. The one that murdered for curiosity.

CHAPTER TWENTY-TWO

THE WIND PICKED up as I made my way down the trail and deep thunder rumbled in the mountains. The night beginning to give way to the dawn as the sun desperately tried to peek through the collapsed pass and storm clouds.

I thought I could smell rain on the air; years of riding and you get used to those signs. Seemed fitting that it would end in lightning and water.

Torches and lamps still burned, but I could see weariness taking its hold on David Weber and his men, most of them slouched against whatever would hold them, rifles cradled to their chests while they smoked.

I watched all of it through George Weber's rifle, like an eagle waiting for the right moment to present itself. Hadn't seen any sign of Jake yet, and that was the only reason I hadn't started removing men from their lives. Couldn't have them killing him before I reached him. Wasn't much of a code or a creed I lived by, but if I promised you something, I would follow through with it. I was about to give up and decide to search for myself when Jake was ushered out of the saloon.

His legs were in irons, one eye swollen shut, and a few cuts and bruises here and there. Lamb followed him, his eyes panning against the dark, white buffalo skin making him look like some sort of specter come back from the other world.

"COVINGTON!" Lamb's grisly voice rang as it was carried on the wind. This was a man I could respect if Fate wasn't angling to have us pull our pieces and see which was the better man.

"I KNOW YOU'RE WATCHING! KNOW YOU'RE LISTENING! YOU COME ON DOWN, NOW. COME ON DOWN AND WE WON'T KILL YOUR FRIEND!"

Jake said something to him, probably cursing the very moment he met me. Lamb backhanded him and left a new bruise across his head.

I thought about putting one between Jake's eyes; it would have taken Lamb's satisfaction and at least let Jake die with some dignity. A weary sigh escaped my chest as I stood. Must have looked like a bloody and dark animal rising from the hunt as I climbed down the ladder of the Graverange hotel. Looks like I'd finally be walking to Trail's End. All paths led there eventually, but I was going to make sure that Lamb and Weber walked with me.

"I'm here, Night Rider."

Iron was drawn and they faced the darkness of the alley as I walked out of it. A few men shrank back even as I smiled like I hadn't a care in the world. "Don't waste your shots, gentlemen. I could have planted you ages ago."

My smile disappeared as I looked at my companion, chains clutching at his legs and hands. "Jake, you alright?"

The man gave a ghost of a smile, gums bleeding from the beating he had taken. "Walking tall, Salem. Craft and his boys hit harder."

Good man. Laugh in the face of death; it's the only way to stave off the fear.

Lamb cut me off. "Enough. Put your weapons down, Salem, nice and slow."

I smirked at him, letting my hand dangle close to my Gun. "Way I see it, Lamb, none of these can hit me, same as this rifle I'm holding can't hit you. Why don't we settle this the way men used to, before the war, and before you and I both did things that has God crying in heaven?" It was bait, I didn't know if I could outdraw the man, but if I could Jake and I might live to see this town behind us.

Lamb smiled; it was the same one I'd seen his spirit giving me a few months back on my trip to the other side, the same one that folks around Andersonville had seen when he darkened their doorstep with his knives.

"Don't think so, Covington. You're not going to live through this. David, you and your men restrain him. Don't worry about his Gun; he wouldn't dare shoot at you while I have him dead to rights."

Smart man, maybe smarter than me. He was damn right about my odds; if I drew on Weber and his lot, I was dead. If I stayed still, I was dead.

Something tickled at my neck, like the whisper of some lost tale on the wind, and I had the urge to look up. Maybe I was looking up to see the heaven that was denied me. Didn't see heaven, but what I did see put a grin on my face just the same. Clouds twisted and turned like a kid playing with thick globs in a mud puddle. A tip appeared, like a finger descending.

"Shouldn't have killed my teacher, Lamb. He taught *me*, he trained *me*. He was a good man, a spiritual leader of his people." I grinned savagely. "And he's decided to help me one more time."

A few men screamed as the twister touched at the end of the valley, burying itself deep into the snow of the pass, twirling it around and blanketing the wind in white . . .

Then it started for the town.

It broke whatever spirit was holding most of these men together. A few ran, looking for cover, not realizing that this whole town was going to be leveled.

"COME BACK, YOU COWARDS!" Lamb shouted at them and his distraction was just what I needed.

My Gun flashed in my hand and I fired direct, but the wind caught my bullet and what I was sure had been a heart shot buried itself in the Sheriff's forearm. He screamed and stumbled back. I aimed again.

"COVINGTON!" David Weber's cry reached my ears. He shuffled toward me. It looked like he had indulged in the drink overnight.

"Did you kill my bro—" He paused when he saw the string of fingers around my neck and his brother's 'sly eye' peaking from my breast pocket.

David tried to raise his rifle, but I planted a bullet between his legs. The man went down howling like a cat, cradling the tattered remains of his manhood.

Men screamed as the twister hit the edge of town, shredding a butcher's stand and sending bits of meat flying across the street. The wind whipped at us and I fought to keep my feet as bits of wood and snow flew past.

A horse ran in panic, trying to get away from the cyclone, knocking into me and sending me stumbling for purchase. I expected to feel a bullet in my back any second, but when I turned to finish Lamb, I found him holding his limp arm tight against his vest, spreading dark splashes across the already red material.

His Gun was trained directly on me and mine was trained on him.

The Night Rider and Black Magpie, ready to see who was the better man.

With destruction and death surrounding us, we both twitched, eyeing each other. I felt the sweat on my brow despite the cold. It had been a while since I stared down death, vulnerable to its touch.

I saw Lamb's finger twitch, right before Jake wrapped the chains binding his hands together around his throat. Lamb's Gun roared but the bullet missed. Mine found its mark, striking him in the lower stomach, a gout of red mist flying into the wind.

Lamb sprawled into the mud, his strength fading as Jake straddled him, pressing the chains down into his neck. I didn't bother trying to intercede; I let Jake become a killer all his own.

Lamb's face turned red, then purple, blood coughing up between his desperate breaths, nails carving deep into Jake's skin. I heard something snap and then a rattle as Lamb's head fell back into the mud, his eyes staring off into oblivion.

The tornado was coming. It had been dancing and weaving on the outskirts of Graverange, eager to scare and give me the edge, but now that Lamb was dead it hungered.

I could barely keep my footing as I grabbed Jake by the shoulders, aiming at his leg irons. "Let's go, Jake!"

The Gun . . .

My brother's weapon was within my grasp. I'd spent years watching my back, waiting for a bullet from Fate. I scrambled across the ground, my own weapon held tight, urging me to reunite it with its brother.

"Salem! SALEM!" Jake hollered at me, but I ignored him, desperately scrambling on all fours like I was an addict after laudanum. The Gun seemed to fly through the air, closer to the tornado every time I was within reach.

The livery was gone; the tornado had chewed through the wood, sending the material flying through the air. Wasn't more than a hundred yards away now, coming towards us.

"For God's sake, man!" Jake sounded like he was near me, close behind. I would have told him to run and look to his own if my mind wasn't focused entirely on my brother's weapon. I reached for the grip, the ivory handle gleaming.

Should have expected it, should have seen it coming. With as much chaos and debris flying around, I should have known Fate would throw something at me.

As my hand closed around the gun, a large wooden slat from the destroyed livery came flying and hit me across the chest. The air was knocked out of me and I went sprawling on my back. I took a deep gasp of air trying to suck in the coolness like a man dying of thirst and I reached for my brother's gun, just out of reach.

Jake appeared and grabbed the Gun from the ground, crouching next to me and pulling at my jacket. "I've got the damn gun! Now let's go!"

My eyes darted to the weapon in his hand and if I could have wept for him I would. He couldn't hear it now, probably because he was panicking, but it would come. The whispers always came.

He reached out a hand for me and I took it. We stumbled down the street as fast as we could, his injuries and mine hindering our speed. We passed Lamb's body, rolling over like it was a fat worm in the mud. His eyes were still open, practically bulging from his head, but they looked confused . . .

Wondering how we had gotten the best of him.

The wind took him and the corpse went flying into the air, joining the rest of the debris as it swirled around the column of wind.

Folks ran every which way, trying to avoid death just the same as us. Tornado could kill me even if a bullet couldn't. We weren't going to make it.

Jake gave me a grin that could have matched my own, swollen eye opening just barely. "Looks like not even you could outshoot the Lord."

Would have agreed with him if the wind hadn't died at that moment. The two of us turned in time to watch the twister disappearing back up to join the clouds, whatever had driven it sated.

CHAPTER TWENTY-THREE

GRAVERANGE WAS A RUIN; tornado had destroyed the livery, butcher stand, and the train station that had been under construction, eagerly awaiting the Pacific lines from California.

Didn't doubt that a few would try to make a go of it, try to salvage their town after the disaster that came upon it. Wouldn't matter in the end; this burg would be a ghost town come the new year.

Wood cracked under our boots as Jake and I surveyed the damage. The clouds had parted and the new dawn was coming through to warm the valley. I saw a few men drift from their hiding holes only to duck back in just as quick, not wanting to test to see if we'd kill them for their part in the previous night.

"Well, you got them all. Feel like you imagined?"

I grunted, doing my best not to look like I was eyeing the Gun in his hand. "This isn't the first time I've ran a man to ground for revenge, Mr. Howe."

"First time you've done it partnered up with someone, I reckon."

Had a point that I couldn't deny, but it didn't feel right. I'd only watched four of them die. Last I had seen of David Weber, he'd been clutching the tattered ruins of his pecker and howling loud enough he could have drowned out a twister. I wasn't leaving until I was sure he was riding the black and I could collect something from him and August Lamb both.

We hadn't had luck on finding either of them.

"Think we should call it, Salem. I'm near dead on my feet." As if to remind me, he yawned and then looked at the Gun in his hand, like it was the first time he was really noticing. "You were awfully keen on this thing, willing to risk that twister to get it. Sorry I've been holding onto it all night." He offered the Gun to me, no guff or strings attached.

My own weapon whispered for me to put a bullet in him and finally take it. My right hand tightened around my weapon's grip and I saw Jake look in confusion, eyes questioning me. It wasn't long before I took my hand away, barely a blink of the eye or the exhale of a breath, but it was too long for me.

A great many thoughts of murder can cross a man's mind in those small moments.

"Why don't you actually try letting go of that Gun, Jake? Without me taking it from you. Go on, just put it in my hand."

I held my hand out, already knowing what was going to happen. Jake reached to give me the weapon, but stopped at the last second, looking down at it, lips thinning and his eyes twitching at the edges.

"I . . . come to think of it, I think I wouldn't mind . . . "

I withdrew my grip and caught his gaze. "Don't bother trying to make excuses. I know you can't give it up, same as I couldn't give mine up. Virgil couldn't either. That was the deal we made all those years ago."

I reached out and squeezed his shoulder. It was all

I could do to comfort him really. "We each promised a river of souls and I've done my fair share of killing. How many does it say you've got left?"

Jake Howe looked down at the Gun and in that moment, I was reminded of my brother, younger, alive, looking down at his newfound weapon like it had the power to grant us all the gold in the world. And just like Virgil, Jake was amazed at how many people he still had to put down.

"Nine thousand, six hundred, and eleven . . . that's what it's whispering to me." Higher number than mine. Guess Lamb had done better at resisting that urge than I had.

"What happens? If you kill the rest, what happens then?"

Hard thing to tell him that his soul was forfeit unless he followed through, but those were the terms we had set; whoever picked up the Gun worked to keep their soul.

"You get to go to Heaven, get your soul back and absolved of all their murders. You get to walk up to the pearly gates blameless. If you die before sending those folks off to their maker, old age or otherwise . . . it's the fire."

Hard thing to find out, realizing you're damned, and Jake wasn't any different. His face went pale, swollen eye widening as his mouth trembled. I wondered if he'd ask if I was lying, if it was another trick, a bit of misdirection to make him hand over the weapon.

"Until then, like me, you can't be killed by most guns. Rifles, pistols, shotguns, you're going to be wading through gunfire like you're old Stonewall himself."

Jake looked at the weapon in his hand. His fingers were curled around his Gun, and through the panic, I was beginning to see his mind turn, the possibilities of what this could mean beginning to mingle with the whispers of power.

"Stonewall died from a gun, Salem."

I nodded. "That he did, just like you can die from a gun. One in particular." My fingers tapped against my holster and I let him in on the immutable fact. "This one here is the only weapon in the world that can plant you."

Silence came between us. I'd already made my peace with it, but I could see Jake wondering, questioning. Could he kill me before I put one between his eyes?

The Gun was probably whispering, urging him on, kill me and he'd be unstoppable. I was prepared if he gave in, I'd been prepared since a shared campfire with my brother so many years ago.

"You planning on killing me, Salem?"

Not today, Jake. When the future came calling, but not today. "No, Mr. Howe. I don't plan on killing you. Consider this my attempt to believe Fate might have other plans for us."

A groan came from a pile of wood close to a barn that had partially collapsed. I glanced at Jake and nodded my head. A grin split my face, a sadistic joy flowing through me.

"I'll explain Fate's design another time. I believe this is who we were looking for."

David Weber crawled out from underneath the wood, a trail of blood leaking out of him. He looked too pale, not long for the world without help. "Please . . . " he panted, clutching at the dirt and reaching out a hand for Jake. "I need help."

The sun was at our backs and all he saw were two dark figures. I glanced over at Jake and offered David's life to him.

"I imagine he gave you that beating. Reckon you've got the hankering to give him something worse in return."

I handed my knife to him; the only thing I was going to collect was the beautiful memory of Jake's first time. Wasn't often you saw the beginning of a man like me.

David screamed when Jake slid the blade under the man's brow, slowly cutting into the flesh, thick red globs of blood staining his screaming face as he cried into the mud. Sinew tore and David's agony reached a crescendo as Jake wrenched with one hand and the man's scalp tore free. David moaned, but the life left him quick enough.

Jake stood back up, panting, looking at the Gun in his left hand and the scalp in his right.

I patted him on the shoulder. "Nine thousand, six hundred, and ten to go."

CHAPTER TWENTY-FOUR

WE RETRIEVED DEAD BEAR'S coffin and found Soldier and Maestro eating serenely on the outside of town, even managed to find a Stagecoach; OVERLAND MAIL emblazoned on the side. Easy enough to hitch my beasts up and head toward the clear pass, aiming for Oklahoma, Texas after.

I managed to salvage most of my collection from where the avalanche had destroyed my previous stage. Jake was silent as he watched me dig through my accouterment. I kept an eye on him, hard not to when he was holding the only thing that could kill me.

We didn't talk much over the weeks it took to get to Oklahoma. The Wichita Mountains rose like giant tombstone markers. Fitting considering my purpose here.

There was an opening of a canyon and sunlight flickered across the rock face above us, pushing the shadows to the ground.

"Stay here, Mr. Howe. You never had much respect for him in the first place."

Jake raised his hands to show he wasn't going anywhere. I dismounted and unhooked Dead Bear's coffin from the back of the stage, letting it drop to the ground with a thud.

He had been quiet since Graverange, hadn't seen hide nor hair of him on the prairie. I had a feeling he'd gone and crossed over, joined the hunting grounds. Opening up the coffin would tell me what I needed to know. I took a deep breath, unsure of what to expect, and I lifted the lid.

The smell hit me first. Rot and ruin had begun to set in upon my teacher. Death had descended as his soul had left. I smiled when I realized that he hadn't ridden to those sacred lands alone. His body was clad in the fur of a white buffalo and a bright sheriff's star gleamed from where it was clutched in his hands.

I smiled, leaning in to whisper to him. "You gave me something to collect from him after all." The hand seemed to uncurl, the skin retracting slightly from his lips, like the ghost of a dead smile as I took the sheriff's star from his hand. I pinned it to my chest, the metal badge adding a tiny weight and giving me more than small satisfaction.

The shadows parted in that canyon as I traversed its path, the things in gloom not daring to show themselves as I passed them. Didn't know exactly what I was looking for, but when I turned a corner and saw the small crevasse, a pile of rocks next to it, I knew it had been prepared for me.

Dead Bear fit easily inside. I felt the tears drip down my face as I placed the rocks around the entrance, burying him the old way, praying a prayer over him that he'd be found worthy and honored on the other side.

I placed the last stone, wiped the tears from my

face, and gripped the Gun again, letting it whisper words of murder into my mind. I tipped my hat to my mentor. "Thank you for my lessons, teacher. Thank you for taking on two wayward souls. I'll ride with you again, when the time comes."

I walked out of the canyon and didn't look back. My oath was fulfilled and I still had so much to do.

Querido wasn't much; just a cantina and a few buildings that I assumed weren't anything other than an old general store and barn. A small chapel sitting at the edge of the road finished off the town.

Jake clutched the wood of my new stage hard as he pulled under the sign proclaiming the town's name and how many people chose to call it home. I would have been nervous too if I had spent so much time away from this beautiful senorita.

I brought the horses to a halt outside the cantina. Music drifted out of the gloom behind the swinging doors, but I didn't hear any singing. Could be she had long since moved on or some old bandito had spirited her away.

I felt a great swell of sorrow for any man that had taken Catarina from this place now that Jake had the means to take whatever he wanted in the lawless regions of the country.

"Worried, Mr. Howe?"

Jake's eyes were riveted to the swinging doors. He clutched David Weber's deputy star in his hand and I knew what was happening in his head. Morality and conscience struggling with the new reality of what he was.

"Don't fight yourself on it, all men are killers at heart. We have been ever since paradise. No one is good when it comes down to it, just takes longer for some to see it."

My companion took a deep breath. I hadn't been trying to comfort him; there wasn't any to be found now. Comfort would come in time, when he realized that he had few choices.

"Go on and find your senorita, Jake. You'll feel better after a poke, guaranteed."

Jake chuckled wearily as he dismounted from the stage, looking up at me and shaking his head. "Going to miss these chats, Salem, but can't say I'll miss the journey. Probably a whole lot less folks eager to kill me to get to you."

I shrugged and pointed at the Gun on his hip. "As long as you're holding that thing, you'll find a whole lot of people trying to kill you for their own reasons."

Jake nodded, licking his lips and suddenly getting serious. "You really believe that next time we meet we'll be trying to plant each other?"

"Yeah, yeah I do. When Virgil and I signed the contract we didn't believe it. Look how that turned out."

Jake shook his head slightly, letting me know that he didn't think it was true, bullshit of the highest quality. "I'm not your brother."

"Yeah," I responded. "I hope you're not."

"Where are you intending to head from here?"

To that I gave a knowing smile. "I have unfinished business with someone. Best not to ask too many questions, though. You'll get answers you won't like."

He might have been about to ask those same

questions before a voice like honey came dripping from the shadows of the cantina. "Jake?"

Her hair fell around her like dark waves, her skin was the lightest brown, and her voice that had been laced with curiosity turned to joy when Jake turned, his eyes filling with delight.

She ran to him and he wrapped her up, as good a time as any to take my leave. "Mr. Howe, I believe you're owed."

Jake raised one hand, smiling broadly as I tossed the sack of gold to him.

"Still standing, Mr. Howe, and with a bag of gold in your hand, Senorita on your arm too. Go become a Don and let's pray we don't meet again."

Catarina looked confused, but Jake nodded and tipped his hat to me. "Good fortune to you, Mr. Covington."

I tipped my hat back to him and flicked the reins. The stage began to move, and the last I saw of Jake Howe, he was enfolded in a deep kiss in the streets of Querido.

I'd tracked my quarry to this little end of nowhere. The sign at the edge of the town said Rattleflats, and it was nothing but four buildings and a silver mine. I ushered my stage across the sandy dunes and pulled into the middle of the square. Folks were watching me, but didn't seem to be running off to tell my prey that I'd come calling.

Made my trail right for the saloon. Word had it my prey worked there, under a different name, but two bounty hunters had already had their wicks blown out trying to cash in on the wanted posters' likeness.

This was revenge for me, not reward.

Barkeep didn't try to stop me as I headed up the stairs. The whores parted when they saw my Gun held tight in my hand. I could hear her in that last room, negotiating with whoever was trying to acquire her services.

"Take me with you, I can't stay here anymore. It wasn't murder, it—"

I gave the door one swift kick and shattered it. The man she was talking to was a thin thing, probably meant to murder him too once they were out on the trail.

"HEY! I DON'T KNOW WHO YOU THINK YOU ARE, FRIEND, BUT—"

My Gun found his kneecap. He'd live, maybe even have a story to tell about me.

The woman fell to her knees, hands clasped tight, begging . . .

I grinned and felt the devil behind it, tipped my hat, and pointed my Gun directly at her head.

"Hello, Miss Holloway."

THE END

ABOUT THE AUTHOR

Wile E. Young is from Texas, where he grew up surrounded by stories of ghosts and monsters. During his writing career he has managed to both have a price put on his head and publish his southern themed horror stories He obtained his bachelor's degree in History, which provided no advantage or benefit during his years as an aviation specialist and I.T. guru.